DIRTY LOVE

BETHANY WINTERS

TRIGGER WARNING

This is a dark romance about two stepbrothers who *are* brothers in every way except blood.

THE FOLLOWING CONTAINS SPOILERS
If you're comfortable going in completely blind,
please feel free to skip to the next page.

Certain aspects of this book may be disturbing and/or triggering for some readers, such as: graphic language, explicit sex scenes, underage drinking and drug abuse, homophobia and homophobic slurs, abuse, depression, self harm, violence, attempted sexual assault (not *by* either main character, but *to* a main character), a graphic hate crime (not *by* either main character, but *to* a main character), non-consensual group sex (not *by or to* a main character), and murder.

PLAYLIST

Welcome To The Black Parade by My Chemical Romance
Mind Games by Sickick
Venom by Eminem
Better Off Dead by jxdn
Voices by Motionless in White
Pill Breaker by Trippie Redd, Travis Barker, Machine Gun
Kelly & blackbear
Blood // Water by grandson
Pray by jxdn
Church by Fall Out Boy
La Di Die by Nessa Barrett & jxdn
21 Guns by Green Day
Protector by City Wolf
Throne by Bring Me The Horizon
Alone Together by Fall Out Boy
Infinity by Jaymes Young

Listen on Amazon Music & Spotify

*"I love you as certain dark things are to be loved,
in secret, between the shadow and the soul.
I love you because I know no other way."*
— Pablo Neruda

For the readers who like it dirty.

PROLOGUE

NICKY

Fourteen years old…

I've never seen my brother cry.

Not once in eleven years.

He's only a few months older than me, but he's always been the stronger one. He's the one who protects me from the bullies at school, the one who holds my ears in the dark when the screaming gets too loud, the one who takes the daily beatings so I don't have to.

He's one of the only two people in the world who have ever given a damn about me.

And now he's the only one I have left.

My tears stream over my face and I look down at the small, faded scar on the inside of my left hand, slowly trailing my thumbnail over the spot. I cut myself on a tree in the woods when I was ten and it hurt like hell. My brother brought me home to clean it up and held me while I cried, then he took a knife from the kitchen drawer and cut himself with it, gave himself the exact same scar as mine just to make me feel better.

Remembering that usually helps me cope at times like these, but it's not working right now.

Nothing is working.

My heart feels like it's stuck in my throat and I can't—

"Breathe, Nicky," Kade whispers in my ear, his arms wrapped around me in a tight grip that would probably hurt if I didn't need him so much. "In and out, long and deep, over and over, remember? Copy me."

I nod and fist his hoodie with both hands, desperately trying not to have a panic attack in front of all these people. It's the middle of the night and our house is full of police officers, the blue and red flashing lights blinding us through the windows on the other side of the small living room. There's a picture of our mom on the side table in the corner, taken by our dad the last time we went to the cabin for the weekend. She was pale and thin like me, with long black hair she used to let me play with when Dad wasn't home. Her smile looks fake in the picture—just like it was a lot of the time—but I know she always did her best to pretend for us.

She made us dinner and watched a movie with us before we went to bed tonight, only to be wheeled outside in a body bag a few hours later.

Dead.

Here one minute and gone the next.

Our dad's telling them she was killed by a man in a mask, one who broke into our house and bashed her head against the kitchen counter while he was on his way home from work. He's saying he walked in on him attacking her and chased him out, but then he let him run away so he could try to save his wife from bleeding out on the floor.

I think he's a liar.

Kade thinks so, too, but we don't say anything.

We know better than to do something stupid like that.

I swallow the lump in my throat and look up at Kade, not surprised to find him glaring at the picture in the corner, his jaw tight, his eyes glassy and bloodshot. He looks angry and devastated and wrecked by the loss of our mother, but still, he doesn't cry. He doesn't have a panic attack. He doesn't do *anything* but hold me tight against his chest, gently running his thumb over my hip beneath my hoodie. I focus on that and try to match his breathing like he told me to, in and out, long and deep, over and over…

"Kade. Nicky," someone says quietly, crouching down in front of us to place her hands on our knees. "My name's Veronica. Do you remember m—"

Kade snatches my leg away from her and I lift my feet up to his lap, twisting in his grip to try and get closer to him. She smiles sadly and lifts her hands up in surrender, careful not to touch us this time. She's a police officer like our dad, a blonde haired woman with brown eyes and thin lips. She looks nice enough, I guess, but just because it's her job to protect people doesn't mean she actually does it.

We know that better than anyone.

"I'm so sorry about your mom," she says, but I can't tell if she means it or not. "I can't even imagine what you two are going through right now, but I need you to talk to me about what you saw here tonigh—"

"They didn't see anything, Ronnie," Dad cuts in, standing over us with his arms folded across his chest, his dark eyes bouncing between me and Kade. "They were upstairs the whole time. Only came down after I chased the bastard out the front door. Right, boys?"

His question makes me flinch and I drop my attention to my lap, remembering what Kade said to me before the cops showed up earlier tonight.

We have to lie, Nicky.

Partly because there's a good chance they won't believe us over one of their own, but also because there's a small chance they *will* believe us, send our dad to jail and split us up in the foster system.

That can't happen.

I can't be away from Kade, and this is the only way to ensure we stay together.

Knowing we have no choice but to agree, we nod our heads and he nods back with silent approval, his nostrils flaring slightly at the sight of Kade's arms wrapped around my waist. He doesn't like it when he holds me like this, says it makes us look like faggots, but luckily for us, he won't say anything like that in front of a room full of his own friends.

He guides the blonde lady away from us and I let out a quiet sob, dropping my face down to my brother's shoulder. "Kade..."

"I got you," he whispers, gently rocking me back

and forth with his hand on my cheek, his soft lips brushing the shell of my ear. "You're okay. I got you."

I cry harder and he wipes my stupid tears with his thumb, then he takes his iPod from his pocket and places the headphones in for me. I have my own iPod with my own songs on it, but I like his better and he knows it. His music fills my ears and I close my eyes, curling myself up into a tiny little ball on his lap.

"I love you, Kade."

He squeezes me tighter and slides his fingers through mine, hiding them between my chest and his to ensure Dad doesn't see. "I love you, too, Nicky."

CHAPTER 1

KADE

Eighteen years old...

"Nicky," I growl. "Get the fuck out."

"Five more minutes," he calls, a quiet laugh leaving him when I continue to bang on the door between us. "Go take a piss in the kitchen sink if you're that desperate."

This fucking brat.

I walk away and exit my bedroom, making my way down to the next room over to let myself in. I open the bathroom door from his side and he jumps, almost slipping on the white tiles beneath his feet.

"Dude, *knock* first."

"I did *knock*, you idiot."

He laughs at me again and I pull my cock out to do my business, my shoulders tightening when I catch a peek at his reflection in the mirror above the counter. He's leaning back against the wall in the shower with his dick in his hand and his thumb pressed against the tip, the soapy water falling over his pale chest and abs, his breathing shallow. I narrow my eyes and search his face through the steam surrounding him, unable to stop myself from wondering what he's thinking about.

Is he picturing *them* to get off?

Are *they* the only thing that can make him hard?

Fucking *boys*?

It makes me sick just thinking about it.

So fucking sick.

Just as I think it, his black eyebrows crash in the center and he stares at me, his light gray eyes flashing with something that looks a lot like heat. He traps his bottom lip between his teeth and I blink, only just realizing that if I can see *his* face, he can see mine, meaning he knows I'm watching him.

Look away, you weirdo.

I clear my throat and put my dick away, keeping my back to him while I wash my hands at the sink. I've seen him naked more times than I can count and I've never thought twice about it before, but ever since his big *confession* six months ago, it feels… different.

We're related by marriage, not blood, but we might as well be. Our parents met when we were three years old and we've lived together ever since. We were raised as brothers. My dad is his dad. His mom is my mom.

Was my mom.

She died when we were fourteen and took our hearts

with her, leaving two broken sons to fend for themselves against a father who likes to hit things.

I hate her for dying.

And I miss her so much it hurts.

The faceless woman who gave birth to me lives somewhere in New York with her *real* family, and Nicky's real dad bailed right after our mom pissed on the stick, said he wasn't cut out to be a father and never looked back. We don't resent them for it, though, because if they hadn't left us, our parents wouldn't have met, and I wouldn't have Nicky. He's an annoying little shit and he lives to fuck with me, but I love him and he's mine.

My little brother.

My best friend.

My entire fucking world.

"Kade?"

His raspy voice pulls me back from my thoughts and I shut the water off, feigning indifference while I dry my *very* clean hands. "What?"

Silence follows and I glance over at him, locking my jaw when I catch the stupid look on his face. He's still leaning back in the exact same spot, still holding his dick with his eyes on mine, his grin taunting and smug.

I've been in here too long and the fucker knows it.

The urge to throttle him is there, but I resist the temptation and whip his thigh with a hand towel instead, enjoying the squeal he lets out as I walk back to my bedroom. I shut the door behind me and stalk towards my on-again, off-again girlfriend, squeezing my cock through my boxers while I run my eyes over her naked body. We're *off* right now, *again*, but that didn't stop her from showing up on my doorstep at two in the morning last night, drunk and needy and desperate for a warm body between her legs.

I snatch her ankle and she sucks in a breath, her thighs closing out of instinct when she recognizes the look in my eyes. "I... I thought you weren't in the mood."

I smirk at that, pulling her across to the edge of the mattress to shove her down on her knees.

She's afraid of me, just like everyone else is.

Everyone but *him*.

I take my dick out and she swallows her fear, her hands resting on my hips as she looks up at me through her lashes. "Why won't you talk to me?"

Because I can't stand you.

"Open."

She does as she's told and I run my thumb over the edge of her jaw, secretly wishing she wasn't so... *tanned*. It can't be natural considering it's winter in Maine and below freezing outside, but I know she wouldn't be caught dead with pale skin. She's a superficial bitch with a closet full of shoes, a killer body and an attitude that screams *I'm perfect and I know it*. Blonde hair cut down to her ass, green eyes framed by thick, artificial eyelashes, bright red lips, coffin shaped nails...

The complete opposite of everything I want.

I shake that off and make do with what I've got, pulling her bottom teeth down with my thumb to slip my dick inside and down to her throat. She chokes on it and I tip my head back on my shoulders, fucking her face with my mouth parted, eyes closed, my thoughts drifting some place I wish they wouldn't.

So fucking sick.

CHAPTER 2

NICKY

I can hear her gagging.

The sound grates on my fucking nerves, my back teeth grinding together while I listen to him abuse her throat like she's his own personal fuck toy.

She's not *his* anything and he knows it.

No longer in the mood to get off, I let go of my cock and step out of the shower, snatching my towel from the counter to wrap it around my waist. The sound continues as I brush my teeth and dry my face, louder now thanks to the lack of water running in here. A few more minutes pass before her pathetic cries echo through the wall between us, making me smile.

Maybe he'll *actually* choke her to death this time.

Hopefully.

Once I'm done drying off, I pull on a black pair of ripped jeans and a gray hoodie, pulling my sleeves down to my knuckles to cover the faint scars on my arms. I don't mind Kade seeing them all the time, but I always hide them from everyone else, afraid they'll laugh at me for the things I like to do to myself behind closed doors.

Kade would never laugh at me.

Not for that.

Forcing myself to smile at my own reflection, I pocket my phone and then walk out to the hall, accidentally bumping right into Arianna Summers on my way to Kade's room. Her cheeks are stained with black streaks of mascara, last night's lipstick smeared all over her mouth, her blonde hair a tangled mess…

I hate her.

She sneers like she heard me and I sidestep out of the way, shoving my hands into my pockets while I watch her disappear around the corner. She may or may not run into our dad on her way out of here, but I know he won't lay a hand on her, wouldn't dare jeopardize his *upstanding member of the community* image for a taste of the *it girl* of Bayford High.

My brother's emo music fills my ears and I walk along to his bedroom, leaning my shoulder against the doorframe while I wait for him to notice me. He's sitting down on the edge of his bed with his eyes on his phone, his elbows resting on a muscular pair of thighs that make mine look like chicken legs. I'm not that skinny, but I'm not Kade Rivers, either. He's a whole ass head taller than me, bigger and harder and *meaner.*

Like now, for example, he knows I'm standing here like a loyal puppy waiting for his master to say *come,* but he pays me no attention because he's an asshole.

It's one of the things I love most about him.

His dark brown hair hangs over his piercing blue eyes and he rakes his fingers through it, his other thumb still scrolling away on the screen in his hand. Losing patience, I make a point to clear my throat and he hides a cocky little grin, finally lifting his head to look at me from beneath his lashes.

"What?"

"I saw Arianna just now," I inform him. "You made her cry."

He laughs at that, but it's not a nice laugh. "And?"

"Did you even get her off after?"

"No," he answers, tossing his phone down on the bed. "She ran away from me before I could offer."

I snort and push myself off the doorframe, not missing the way his body tenses up with every step I take towards him. I smirk to myself and pick up the phone, feigning innocence while I scroll through his playlist. I choose *Mind Games* by Sickick and drop down on his bed beside him, leaning back against his headboard with my arm folded behind my head. He gives me a slow, deliberate once over and then looks away, standing up to grab some clothes from the free standing closet in the corner. He's still wearing nothing but his boxers, unashamed of the small scars and bruises covering his tanned back—some new and some not so new, some from our dad and some not.

"Are you getting back together with her?"

"I don't fuckin' know."

"How can you not know?" I roll my eyes, hating the fact that his sheets still smell like her disgustingly sweet perfume. "You don't even like her."

"Nicky…" he warns, and even though he's got his back to me, I can tell he's speaking through his teeth.

"What?"

"Quit talking about fucking Arianna," he orders, still avoiding my eyes as he moves for the shower. "I'll be five minutes. Stay there and wait for me to get out."

"Whatever you say, Daddy," I mutter, barely even flinching when he stops mid step and fists the collar of my hoodie, ripping me off the bed to shove me back against the wall next to his nightstand.

His actions would scare the ever loving shit out of anybody else, but I just lift my chin like the brat he calls me, grinning with my tongue pulled between my teeth, my heart racing with adrenaline.

I knew this was coming.

I was waiting for it—*looking forward* to it, even.

I know he wanted to strangle me in the bathroom for acting up the way I did before, and I know for a *fact* he was only hard back there because of me. I saw the way he tried to hide it behind his hand when he walked out. Watching me in the shower made him hot, had him running back to his ex-girlfriend to let her finish him off, the stupid whore.

I really do hate that girl.

His eyes bounce between mine and he glares, looking down at me with his hand wrapped around my throat, his fingertips digging into my flesh. "I'm not him," he says slowly, still hung up on the *Daddy* thing, I'm guessing.

I'm aware my current situation should say otherwise, but I don't call him out on it. Partly because I know he'd never hurt me like that, but mostly because I like him like this—his undivided attention on me and *only* me, his huge body pinning mine, his mouth so close I can practically *taste* him… it makes me sick but it also makes me fucking crazy.

"I never said you were."

"Then why—" he cuts off, changing his mind. "Why you bein' a little bitch right now?"

"I'm not bein' a bitch."

"Nicky, I swear to g—"

"Because you let her in here!" I blurt out, dropping my head back against the wall with a soft thud. "You spend less time with me when you're with her."

"I spend *all* my time with you, baby brother," he stresses. "It's *always* me and you."

"Except at night," I argue, unable to stop myself. "When she's in your bed instead of me."

His jaw ticks and he tightens his grip around my neck, causing an involuntary sound to leave my throat. It's desperate and needy, and I can't help the way I'm damn near *writhing* between him and the wall. My hard dick brushes his thigh and he glares again, opening his mouth like he's about to say something about it, but he doesn't get the chance before our dad's newest girl-friend appears in the open doorway.

Oh, fuck.

"*Kade!*" she screeches over the music. "What on earth are you doing? Get off him!"

He releases me like I burned him and takes a full step back, still staring at me from beneath his dark eyelashes, his chest rising and falling with slow, deep breaths. He's not afraid of getting into trouble. He's only afraid of her seeing something she shouldn't, something that would ruin us both and tear us apart.

Elle's eyes land on me and she offers me a *look*, one that suggests she did me a favor or some shit. "Are you okay, Nicky?" she asks, patronizing as fuck.

She thinks I'm a pussy, just like everyone else does.

Everyone but *him*.

I ignore her stupid question and she sighs, nodding to herself while she smoothes her hands over the front of her floral dress. She's an average looking blonde woman in her late twenties—a prissy little bitch who's closer to our age than our dad's. They've been together for a few months now and I'm sure he just *loves* how tight her pussy is, but we have no intention of being nice to her and she knows it.

"We're leaving for church in fifteen minutes," she informs us, attempting to sound authoritative but failing. "Please dress appropriately and don't be late."

We continue to ignore her and she hesitates, almost as if she doesn't want to leave us alone together, but then Kade turns his head to look at her and she drops her eyes, her heels tapping along the hardwood floors in the hall as she makes a beeline for the bathroom.

"I don't like her, Kade."

He nods and leans over to snatch the clothes he dropped before he grabbed me. "I know."

"Kade—"

"Drop it, Nicky," he cuts in, barely sparing me a glance as he shoulder checks me on his way to the shower.

"Asshole."

"What?"

"Nothing," I chuckle, grabbing some clean sheets from the linen closet to get to work.

FIFTEEN MINUTES LATER, WE'RE BOTH DRESSED IN DARK jeans and long sleeved shirts, walking downstairs to find our dad sitting at the kitchen island, a cigarette pinched between his teeth with his eyes on the phone in his hands. Elle's standing beside him with her arms crossed over her chest and a troubled look on her face, but it seems he's only half interested in whatever she's saying to him.

"...for goodness sake, he had his hand wrapped around Nicky's throat," she hisses. "He was *choking* him, Eric."

"They're just boys being boys, Elle," he says distractedly, dabbing his roach into the ashtray on the counter. "They fight like that all the time. It's not a big deal."

"No, you didn't see the way they were "

"The way we were what?" Kade asks, moving for the fridge to grab us two waters.

She wisely shuts her mouth and Dad looks up at us, only just tearing his attention away from whatever he's reading on his phone. The man looks good for his age, his dark hair a little gray at the edges, bright blue eyes similar to Kade's and a nasty temper to match. We're pretty sure he's an actual psychopath, one who has the nerve to look us dead in the eye while we eat breakfast five feet from the spot where he broke our mother's skull.

He killed her right here in this very room, but you wouldn't think it just by looking at him. He's a master at manipulating people, probably enjoys the fact that no one knows he's a cold blooded murderer who hits his own kids. He hasn't hit me since I was little and he's backed off of Kade over the last couple of years, too, probably because he's gotten bigger since he started fighting in the woods when he was sixteen, but he's got no problem hurting us in other ways. Like the time he locked our twelve year old dog outside in the snow, shot her in the back when she barked all day and then forced us to bury her dead body in the back yard.

He has no reasons for the shit he does to us, he's just a sick fuck who gets off on watching people suffer.

"Did you boys see this yet?" he asks us, pulling me from my thoughts. "It's disgusting."

"What is?" Kade mutters, passing me a water before taking a sip of his own.

"This," he says, flipping his phone towards us so we can see. "Last month, a high school teacher was fired not far from here for being gay, remember?"

My brows jump and I look up at him, a tiny, pathetic glimmer of hope rushing through me at the thought of him defending the gay guy, but he soon squashes that like he squashes everything else he touches.

"His story went viral the other day and there are thousands of comments on it, almost half of them backing the fucking teacher and comparing his dismissal to a *hate crime*," he sneers, shaking his head with a scoff. "It's almost as if these people are *willing* to let this faggot corrupt our children with his lifestyle."

I flinch slightly and Kade notices, making a show of shoving his water bottle into the trash to get the attention off me. "We're gonna be late," he points out, tipping his chin at the clock on the wall. "Nicky's riding with me."

"Wait, I thought we could all ride together," Elle calls after us, sighing when we make no move to stop.

"We're going out with the boys right after," Kade lies, neither of us looking back to check our dad's reaction, too afraid he'll find something he won't like. "It'll be easier if we take two cars."

We grab our coats and Kade follows me outside, pulling his keys from his pocket to unlock the shitty black truck that used to belong to our mom's younger brother. He's been in jail for the last few years, because our dad put him there for selling cocaine to teenagers.

Kade could afford something a lot nicer than this if he really wanted to, but I know he's dead set on saving as much money as he can before graduation to get us the fuck out of here.

To get *me* away from *him*.

Him and every other homophobic fucker in this town.

He jumps into the driver's seat and I climb up to sit beside him, turning my head away to wipe the stray tear slipping over my cheek. Keeping my eyes on the heavy downpour outside, I wrap my arms around myself and lift my shoulders up to my ears, shivering at the cold racking through my bones. Kade flicks the heat on for me and drives off towards the church, only grabbing my thigh to yank me over to the middle seat once the house is out of sight. I suck in a breath and let it out slowly, secretly enjoying the way his body feels pressed up against mine. I shiver again and take my cigarettes out to hide it, lighting one up before doing the same for him. He doesn't bother to ask me if I'm okay. He just takes my free hand and links our fingers together, shoving them down between my legs to keep us both warm. Another tear slips out but I let it fall this time, knowing he'll notice if I move to wipe it away.

"You need to stop doing that."

"Doing what?" I ask, already knowing the answer.

"Wearing your thoughts all over your face."

I chew the inside of my cheek and he slows the truck down, turning my chin towards him once we get to the stop light at the end of the street.

"Don't let em' see you, baby brother," he whispers, slowly trailing his cold thumb over the skin beneath my eye. "No one but me, remember?"

I nod once and face forward again, struggling to keep my emotions at bay like he wants me to. It's not as easy as he makes it look, but I've had a lot of practice over the years and I can make it happen when I put my mind to it.

We get to the church a few minutes later and Kade pulls up on the side of the road, releasing my hand to jump out into the rain. Several people are huddled up beneath their umbrellas on the street, most rushing to the entrance with their heads down to get inside. I hop down from the passenger side and shove my hands into my pockets, forcing my features even when I spot my dad and Elle pulling up behind us. He doesn't give a shit about the fucking church—or anyone but himself— but he seems to enjoy this shitty town in the middle of nowhere, and showing up here every Sunday is mandatory for his image.

He greets a few people in passing and then falls in line beside me, smiling at a large pregnant woman whose name I've forgotten. "What were you and your brother fighting about earlier?" he asks quietly, shaking her husband's hand before guiding me up the front steps.

I smirk and turn my head to look at him, not missing Kade's intense stare on the side of my face. "He made Arianna cry," I say simply, feigning a cockiness I don't feel. "I told him I could make her scream."

A light laugh leaves him and he claps me on the back of my neck, shaking me like we're *boys* as he walks me through the main doors. "That mouth's gonna get you in big trouble one of these days, kid."

I shrug and he walks away with Elle to say hello to her parents, leaving me alone with Kade and a few of the boys from school. As soon as they're done kissing his ass, I take my seat beside my brother and he pinches my outer thigh, making me jump.

"*Ow.*"

"Fucking please, you little shit," he whispers, but I don't miss the slight grin on his face.

I grin back and turn my attention to the altar at the front, just *thrilled* to learn about all the ways I'm about to burn in hell when I'm done here.

CHAPTER 3

KADE

"THIS GAME'S TOO EASY," Nicky mutters, leaning back against my headboard with his knees spread out wide and his gray hood pulled over his head.

He changed back into his sweats as soon as we got home and he's been quiet ever since, same way he is every Sunday thanks to Father Paul and his bullshit preach about how dirty it is for boys to kiss boys. We don't really *believe* or anything like that, but I know it sucks to feel like he'd be hated by everyone he knows for something he can't change or control.

He *won't* be hated, because he promised me he'll never tell anyone else, but still…

Realizing he's probably cold, I reach over and grab him the throw blanket from the bottom of my bed, lying it out over the bottom half of his body. It's not like we can't afford heat, but our dad'll go off on us if we keep it on all night while he's at work.

"It's not *easy*, Nicky, you're just a fuckin' nerd," I

point out, taking a slice of pizza from the box between us.

He snorts at that, shaking his head at me with a small smile. "Fuck off."

I laugh to myself and keep playing with my free hand, side-eyeing him when he leans over me to grab the half smoked joint from the nightstand. He's practically *lying* on top of me, his chest resting on my abs through our clothes, his soft hair just inches from my face. I tense but he pretends not to notice, staying like that while he takes my lighter to burn the tip. As soon as he's done, he moves back to where he was before and takes a couple long hits, but then the fucker leans over me again to grab the ashtray he forgot the first time. I snatch the collar of his hoodie and shove him back against the headboard, tossing everything he could possibly need on his lap for easy access. He rolls his lips together and looks up at me, bravely holding my eyes as he blows a cloud of smoke out towards my face.

"Thank you," he says, the infuriating little brat.

I make a sound and he laughs at me, rolling his eyes when I steal the joint from his hand and tip my chin at the pizza box. "Eat some more."

"I don't want any more."

"I don't care if you want it or not."

He pouts a little bit and I crook my finger, motioning for him to come closer. He does as he's told and I lift a slice up to his mouth, enjoying the way he opens for me without argument. He takes a bite and I watch him closely, unable to tear my eyes away from his pouty lips while he chews it.

"Good boy," I whisper, not missing the way his breath shakes on an exhale.

I know I shouldn't play with him like this—that I shouldn't play with him *period*—but he barely touches food anymore and it pisses me off.

At least this way I know he's eating, even if it means using his own body against him to make him do it.

As soon as he's finished, I move back and reach for a napkin, freezing when he catches my wrist to stop me. I raise a brow and he hits me with a tiny little smirk, slowly pulling my hand back to his mouth, my fingers brushing the skin just below his lips.

"Nicky…" I warn, but I can't bring myself to tell him no.

My heart is racing and my dick is hard and I'm fucking *dying* to find out what he'll do next.

Still smirking like the goddamn devil in my baby brother's body, he leans up on one elbow until he's facing me fully, then he slips his tongue out and licks the sauce from my thumb, swirling it around to make sure he gets it all. I groan before I can stop it and he takes that as an invitation, dipping his head to take my middle fingers into his mouth.

Fuck.

"Nicky," I rasp, barely recognizing the sound of my own voice. "What the fuck are you doing?"

He doesn't answer that—because he's too busy deep throating my fucking hand—but I swear I can almost *hear* the thought running through his head.

Showing you I can do it better than her.

His teeth graze my knuckles and I'm about to do

something I shouldn't, like pin him down and choke him until he's gagging for me, but then I hear a car door slam outside and snap myself out of it. I rip my fingers from his mouth and jump up to my feet, discreetly adjusting my cock in my jeans as I walk over to the window. I peek through the blinds and look outside, relieved when I realize it's not our dad coming home early, just one of the neighbors across the street.

"Is it him?"

"No," I answer, using the front of my jeans to wipe his saliva from my fingers.

Jesus.

I shake my head to clear it and then walk back over to him, both of us thinking the same thing but never saying it out loud, never giving it a voice.

We push our luck in the dark, when no one's around to witness how fucked up we are beneath the surface.

He looks up at me and wiggles his way out of his hoodie, his smile lazy, his eyes a little bloodshot from the weed.

"You tired?"

He nods and removes the rest of his clothes, his pale body on full display minus the black fabric of his boxers, his left leg hooked over the blanket while he curls himself up into a ball in the middle of my bed.

I should tell him to get out, make him go back to his own room before he passes out in here, but I don't do that. I like it better when he's close to me, which is why I strip down to my underwear and lie down beside him, carefully running my fingers through his hair while I watch him fall asleep.

CHAPTER 4

KADE

"*Boys! Get up! Now!*"

My eyes pop open at the sound of our dad's shouted voice, followed by the front door slamming with enough force to shake the entire house.

"Shit," Nicky whispers from beside me, shooting up in bed like he's actually about to go down there.

Not a chance in hell.

He moves to stand but I move faster, pinning him to the mattress with my hands on either side of his head, my hips resting between his open thighs. "Stay here."

"But—"

"I said *stay here*," I repeat through my teeth, slower this time. "I mean it, Nicky. If you leave this fucking room I swear to god I'll never forgive you."

He swallows and I soften my features for him, gently

pressing a kiss to the creased spot between his eyebrows. Knowing our dad's about to come charging upstairs any second now, I climb out from between my brother's legs and throw a black pair of sweats on, leaving him there while I go downstairs to meet the pissed off fucker in the living room.

"Where were you last night?" he asks, leaning back against the side of the couch with his arms crossed over his chest, still wearing his police uniform from the twelve hour shift he just finished.

"What do you mean?"

"Do not play dumb with me," he warns, straightening up to his full height, pointing toward the bay window beside us. "The neighbor down the street just told me she saw you two walking back here at three o' clock in the fucking morning. In what world are my teenage sons allowed to stay out all night, Kade?!"

"I'm sorry," I lie, hoping to wrap this up quick so I can get back to Nicky. "We went to Arianna's house and fell asleep watching a movie. It was an accident."

"Oh, really?" he asks, his tone light, but I'm not buying it. "You should invite her over for dinner soon. I'd love the chance to get to know her properly."

"Yeah, I bet you would," I mutter, scoffing quietly at the thought because no, that's not happening.

Before I can blink, his huge fist connects with my cheek and I fall over the coffee table behind me. My back hits the floor and I roll over onto my side, lowering my head to hide the way my face is screwed up in agony.

Fucking prick.

"What did I tell you about talking back?!" he shouts, but I can barely hear it over the ringing in my ears.

I'm sure he hits me even harder than he did when I was smaller, almost like he's afraid I'll start fighting back if he doesn't keep me in line. I won't fight back, though, because I'm not stupid enough to believe he won't take it out on Nicky if I push him hard enough.

He'd have to kill me first, but I wouldn't put it past the psychotic piece of shit to do just that.

"Where's your brother?"

"Asleep," I grit out, struggling to keep my tone respectful. "*Sir.*"

But he's not asleep.

I can just imagine him pacing back and forth in my bedroom right now, warring with himself over whether or not he should disobey me.

The thought makes me nauseous.

As if he can hear what I'm thinking, Dad looks over at the stairs and I force myself up to my feet, ignoring the way the room spins in front of me as I move to block his path. He raises a dark brow at that, staring down at me with his head cocked in thought. He's a tall fucker, but I'm almost level with him now and I will *not* let him get by me, especially not when I recognize that hateful look in his eyes.

He thinks Nicky needs to toughen up.

I think *he* needs to swallow a fucking wrench.

One day.

One day, we'll get our revenge on the man who killed our mother and run somewhere far away from here.

Together.

We just have to keep our mouths shut and wait it out.

Knowing I'm not about to move at his command, he laughs cruelly and shakes his head at me, slowly backing away towards the door leading to the kitchen. "You're both grounded for a week."

Like I give a fuck.

As soon as he's gone, I turn around and take the stairs two at a time, stopping just inside my bedroom when I realize Nicky's not in here. I look around and then snap my eyes to the bathroom door, pushing my way inside without knocking because I have to *see* him, to know that he's okay.

He's not okay, though.

He's sitting on the floor with his back against the counter, his pale chest heaving, his eyes filled with pain as he stares at the fresh cuts on his left arm.

Fuck.

Before I can move or react, he looks up at me and lets out a noise that hurts my heart, gritting his teeth as he digs the sharp edge of the razor into his flesh.

"Damn it, Nicky, knock it *off*," I growl, rushing towards him to straddle his bare thighs.

Carefully plucking the blade from his fingers, I toss it into the sink and reach up to wet one of the hand towels on the counter, pressing it to his slashed up arm to stop the bleeding there. He winces at the pressure and I wince, too, forcing myself to calm down before I hurt him even more than he's hurt himself. He hasn't gone as deep as he's gone before, but it still scares the shit out of me all the same.

"You promised me you'd stop," I remind him, unable to hide the strain in my voice. "You *promised*, Nicky."

"I *know*," he chokes out, using his clean arm to hide his face from me. "I'm sorry, I just… it's my head, Kade. My head just *goes* there sometimes and I can't stop it."

I don't understand what he means, but I don't bother saying that out loud, still pressing the towel to his arm while I run my free hand up to the back of his neck. "Two more years," I tell him, gently pulling his hair to force him to look at me. "Two more years and we're gone, remember?"

He sniffs and nods his head a few times, suddenly forgetting his own demons to examine the newest bruise forming on my face. "Does it hurt?"

"No," I lie, but his flinch tells me he knows it does.

"Why won't you let him hit me?"

"Nicky…"

"Jesus, stop looking at me like that," he snaps, slapping my hands away to shove my chest. "I know you don't think I can handle it but I *can*. You think I'm a pussy but I'm *not*. I can fucking take it, Kade."

"But you're not going to!" I snap back, leaning over him to crowd his space. "He will never touch you again because I won't let it happen. And it's not because I think you can't handle it. It's because *I* can't handle watching him hurt you. Watching *anyone* hurt you. It would kill me, Nicky."

His face falls and he wraps his hands around my neck, gutting me all over again when I catch the broken look in his eyes. "It kills me, too, you know?" he whispers, lightly ghosting his lips over the sore spot on my cheek. "*This* fucking kills me."

"Is that why you cut yourself?"

He nods, and I let out a shaky breath, bringing him with me as I move to sit down beside him, sliding my arms around his waist until there's not an inch of space left between us. His body relaxes on top of mine and he clings to me, hiding his face in the crook of my neck with his ankles locked around my back.

"This is not our forever, you hear me?" I ask quietly, glaring at the wall opposite while I run my hands over his spine. "It's not."

CHAPTER 5

NICKY

I WAKE up to Kade shaking me from behind, his hard chest pressed up against my back, his short nails digging into my waist. "Nicky," he croaks out, his voice raspy from sleep. "Nicky, fuck me, turn it off."

"You turn it off."

"It's your fucking phone."

I groan and reach over to hit the stop button on my alarm, pulling my hand back just as quick when the icy cold air hits my flesh. Instead of getting up to get ready for school, I lie back down and pull the blanket up to my chin, shuffling back a bit to seek out his body heat.

"Nicky—"

"It's freezing, Kade," I complain, bravely shoving my ass back into his lap. "Please?"

He hesitates, just like I knew he would, but then he sighs and locks his arms around me, his warm fingers tangled with mine, our joined hands pressed up against my chest. I grin and close my eyes, resisting the urge to roll my hips back on his dick. I know he's as hard as I am because I can feel it digging into the back of my thigh, but I also know better than to move or call him out on it.

A few seconds pass and my mind shuts off again, but then he growls in my ear and stretches over me to grab something from the nightstand.

"You sleep like a fucking dead person," he bites out, shutting my second alarm off before tossing my phone back where he found it.

"You say that like it's a bad thing."

He pinches my ribs and I jolt, quickly snatching his wrist to stop him from doing it again. He spreads his fingers out over my abs and I shiver, but it's not from the cold and we both know it.

"It's not a good thing, Nicky," he tells me, his warm breath hitting the side of my neck. "Someone could come in here and you wouldn't even know it."

"No one's coming in here, brother," I tell him, struggling to hide the obvious heat in my voice. "And even if they did, it doesn't matter because you'd break their hands before they could come near me."

"You think so?"

"I know so," I correct him, rolling over to face him when I feel his eyes on me. "What?"

"What?"

"Why are you staring at me like that?"

He blinks and pulls his brows in, studying my face with something that looks like… I don't know what it is, but I know that I like it, that I want *more* of it.

Just as I move to lie down on his chest, my third

alarm goes off and he grits his teeth, taking my jaw to dig his fingers into my cheeks. "Turn it off for good before I throw it out the fucking window."

I hide a grin and sit up to do as I'm told, tucking my dick beneath my waistband before I reach over to grab my hoodie from the floor. I throw it on and grab the cigarettes from the side, walking over to sit down on the wooden bench seat beneath the window. I crack it open and move the blinds across a little bit, resting my elbows on my knees while I light the end. I blow my smoke out and lean my head against the glass, looking over at Kade when I realize he hasn't moved yet. He's staring at me again, probably remembering the way I sucked his fingers clean before I passed out last night. I forgot about it until just now, but I know he'll only tell me to shut my mouth if I try to talk about it.

"Hurry up with that before you freeze to death," he mutters, standing up to flick the bedside lamp on.

He adjusts his dick in his boxers and I chew my bottom lip, shamelessly watching his body move as he walks for the bathroom. He closes the door behind him and I finish the last of my cigarette, closing the window before outing my roach in the ashtray on the side. I pull my hood over my head and climb back into bed, figuring I've got at least ten minutes while I wait for him to take a shower. I close my eyes and lie down on his pillow, falling asleep almost instantly with his warmth and familiar scent surrounding me. After what feels like three seconds, the bathroom door opens and he rips the blanket from my body, grabbing the backs of my knees to pull my ass to the edge of his bed.

"Shower. Now."

"God fucking *damn it*, Kade, you bossy prick."

He raises a brow at that, his chest and abs still glistening with water, his wet hair sticking out in all directions. I stare at him and he twists the hand towel he's holding, laughing to himself when I jump up and run to the bathroom to get away from him.

"What's the matter, baby brother?"

"Fuck you."

DAD'S STILL NOT HOME FROM WORK BY THE TIME WE LEAVE for school, which is why we've left the truck running on the street for a few minutes, letting it warm up a bit before we head outside to get in. I climb up to the passenger seat and take my spot in the middle next to Kade, not even bothering to worry about what the neighbors will say if they see us like this. I'm sure they talk about us—Officer Rivers' weird sons who spend almost every minute of every day together—but I don't give a shit. I'm not about to distance myself from my older brother to make them happy.

"Can we still get a coffee on the way?" I ask, stealing his phone from his pocket to plug it into the stereo.

Glancing at the clock on the dash, he nods and drives towards the gas station about a mile away from school. I wait in the truck while he heads to the vending machine inside, shaking my head at him when he comes back with two to-go cups and a chocolate chip muffin.

"I'm not hungry," I tell him, already knowing it's for me without having to ask.

"You didn't eat your breakfast."

"I ate half of it," I argue, taking the coffees to hold them while he drives. "Did you already put the sugars in?"

He nods and tips his chin at the brown paper bag on my lap. "Eat."

"No."

"Nicky."

"Make me," I challenge, knowing he'll do it, *hoping* he'll do it the same way he did last night.

He looks at me and raises a brow—his usual response when I'm acting like a brat on purpose—then he snatches the muffin and holds it up to my mouth. Despite the fact I wasn't lying before about not being hungry, I take a small bite and chew it slowly, smirking to myself when I catch the look in his eyes.

I can eat just fine by myself, but I know he likes feeding me just as much as I like being fed by him.

I take another bite and lick both corners of my lips, enjoying the way his eyes drop to follow the movement. I'm just about to fuck with him some more, but then I sigh, disappointed when I realize we're at school already. A shout rings out from somewhere and I look out through the windshield, spotting Mark and a few of the other boys messing around in the parking lot. Kade parks the truck next to his friends and I pass him his coffee, rewrapping the rest of the muffin to shove it into the shelf on the dash. He jumps out and I follow behind him, awkwardly pulling my hood over my head to avoid the stares on me.

We're no better than anyone else here, but they still fear us because Kade's a scary motherfucker with a mean glare and an attitude that screams *stay the fuck away from me*. In their eyes, he's the big man and I'm just his loyal shadow. Nicky Rivers—Kade Rivers' loser baby brother.

I don't mind, though.

I like it here.

I'm *safe* here and I always will be.

"Sup, boys?" Mark tips his chin, bumping Kade's fist before doing the same to mine. "Wanna hit?"

I shrug and move to take the joint from his fingers, stopping when Kade subtly shakes his head no.

No drugs unless they come from me.

I roll my eyes and light another cigarette, leaning back behind the truck to ensure the teachers don't catch us smoking. Kade and I sip our coffees and pass the cigarette back and forth between us, listening quietly while the boys chat shit about the fights this weekend.

"You know who you're fighting yet?" Mark asks Kade, dipping his head to blow his smoke out towards his feet.

"I heard Austin say he's down," Parker jokes, snorting when Austin's eyes widen in horror.

"Man, fuck you, I fought him last weekend," he complains, pointing a finger at the nasty black eye on his face. "See this shit? I'm done for the year. It's somebody else's turn to get their ass beat."

I laugh to myself and flick my roach into the bushes

behind us, doing a double take when I spot the hot guy walking through the parking lot towards the main entrance. He's tall and lean and even paler than I am, dressed in all black from his shoulders to his feet, his icy blond hair covering his eyes and forehead. As if sensing he's being watched, he looks up and gives me a slow once over—a *really* slow one—then he winks at me and carries on walking.

What the fuck?

"Who is that?" Austin asks, quickly stealing the joint from Mark's mouth while he's distracted.

"Not sure," Parker answers, standing up on his tiptoes to look at him over the truck, chuckling to himself while he taps Kade's arm with his elbow. "I bet he'll fight you."

Everyone laughs at that, but Kade doesn't look amused. He's looking at *me*, his perfectly defined jaw locked with a glare that makes me wince.

Shit.

———

"HEY."

I frown and lift my head from my math notebook, finding the new guy standing in front of me in the middle of the busy cafeteria. He's got his ghostly white hands shoved into his pockets, his white hair seeming even brighter up close. I've tried not to look directly at him since Kade caught me checking him out this morning, but we share a couple classes together and I know I've felt his eyes on me more than once.

"Hey," I say back, struggling to maintain eye contact.

"Can I sit here?" he asks, gesturing to the empty bench seat across from me.

"Um… yeah, I guess."

He smiles freely and drops his ass down, leaning in a little too close for comfort with his forearms resting on the table. "I'm Jasper."

"Nicky."

"Yeah, I know," he chuckles, tipping his chin at something behind me. "That Kade guy everyone's afraid of. You're his… friend?"

My brows dip at his strange question and I look over my shoulder, grinding my teeth together when I find him talking to Arianna in the middle of the lunch line, his eyes narrowed, her bony little hand wrapped around his arm like she owns him.

"I'm his brother."

"You're his *brother*?" Jasper echoes, scrunching his nose as if the fact confuses him, but then he cocks his head in thought. "Wait, aren't you both seniors? Are you twins or something?"

"Stepbrothers," I mutter, forcing myself to tear my eyes away from Kade and his ex-girlfriend. "He's three months older than me."

"Oh," he says, nodding to himself with yet another chuckle. "Right, okay. That makes more sense."

"What's that supposed to mean?"

He shrugs and opens his mouth to answer, but then he looks up at something over my head and leans all the way away from me, almost like it's a natural instinct, his expression quickly changing from light to wary. Kade sits down beside me and hands me a sandwich and a bottle of water, his dark eyes never leaving the guy sitting opposite us. Beneath the table, he locks his ankle around mine and I'm quick to obey, silently sliding closer to him without hesitation. Jasper's pale blue eyes bounce between us and I drop mine to my lunch, anxiously picking at the corner of my sandwich.

What the hell is he *staring* at?

"Was that your girlfriend?" he asks Kade, raising a cocky ass brow like a brave fucker.

Instead of answering him, Kade tilts his head and uncaps his water, his impatience clear.

"Okay, then," Jasper mouths, lightly tapping the table with his fist as he moves to stand. "Good talk, man."

I roll my lips together and he winks at me again, seemingly unbothered by the glare on his back as he walks toward the door on the other side of the room.

"Maybe they just wink a lot where he's fro—"

"Shut up, Nicky."

"Okay."

CHAPTER 6

KADE

Friday night, we drive out to the woods and park beside the long row of cars lined up next to the gate, ignoring the rusted chains and the signs warning us not to trespass. We could get into a lot of trouble for this, especially considering what we're doing out here almost every weekend, but we've been coming for years now and no one's been caught yet.

Once I've helped Nicky climb over the six foot fence, we take the old path towards the abandoned church about a half a mile away, following the sound of the music blaring in the distance. Just behind the rotting building, there's a small clearing between the trees, filled with high school kids and college students walking around with solo cups filled with cheap beer. The spot we use is just a sunken pit of land, surrounded by a few logs people sit on to drink, get high and watch the bloodshed.

The guy who runs these things was a little spooked

to have me at first considering I'm the son of a well known cop, but it didn't take long for me to earn my place here and prove I'm no snitch.

Mark and the boys catch up to us and I look around, finding Skully talking to a group of guys by the campfire, probably closing the last of his bets before it's my turn to fight. He's a scrawny little shit with dark curly hair cut down to his shoulders, and even though he knows he's too old to keep partying with a bunch of high school kids, he needs the cash to make rent and put himself through college, same way *I* need the cash to get me and Nicky someplace far away from here.

I can't get a real job yet, mostly because I can't be away from Nicky for hours at a time, but also because our dad doesn't want us to be independent like that. He doesn't want us to leave this shit town in a few months like we're planning to. He wants us trapped here under his thumb, for us to stay like that until we're old enough to join the police academy like he did. He wants to control us in every way possible, and I'll be damned if I sit back and do nothing to stop him.

I'll fight a hundred grown ass men if that's what it takes to protect my little brother.

"Yo, Kade," Skully calls once he spots me, walking over to clap me on the back. "Sup, baby Rivers?" he jokes, ruffling Nicky's hair beneath his hood.

My jaw ticks and I grab his shoulder to push him back a step, making a point to remove his hand from Nicky's head. "Don't do that."

"Sorry," he chuckles, tossing me the bag I texted him

for earlier, waving me off when I take my wallet out to pay him. "Forget about it, man. This one's on me."

I shake my head and slip him the cash, just like he knew I would because we don't take handouts from anyone. Nicky takes the coke from my hand and I snatch it back, glaring at him from beneath my lashes while I dip my head to take a hit. Once I'm satisfied it's not poison, I hand it over and he smiles to himself, shoving my key into the bag to snort his own hit. He wipes his nose with his sleeve and I scan the crowd to look for the college senior Skully managed to set me up with tonight, fucking *itching* to rid all this pent up energy inside me.

"Where is he?"

"Over there," Skully answers, tipping his chin at the blond haired, quarterback looking guy who just so happens to be talking to my ex-girlfriend. "His name's Avery. He's, uh… he's cocky, you know?"

I smirk at that, raising a brow when I catch Nicky sneaking another hit of coke behind my back. Skully moves to talk to the guy I'm fighting and I take the opportunity to grab my brother, roughly snatching the collar of his hoodie to yank his chest to mine.

"You think I can't see you?" I ask quietly, leaning over him until our noses are almost touching.

The little brat just grins, his hot little tongue trapped between his teeth, his gray eyes shining with something that looks an awful lot like defiance. My nostrils flare and I pull him along with me, shoving his ass down on one of the logs next to the boys where I can keep an eye on him.

"Don't fucking move."

He grins some more but I ignore it, looking over when I catch Arianna practically throwing herself at the guy on the other side of the circle, staring at *me* over her shoulder while she trails her fingernail over Avery's chest. She's been acting like this for weeks now, constantly trying to rile me up or make me jealous or some shit, but what she keeps failing to realize is that I don't give a damn about her or who she's fucking.

The only fucks I have to give are for Nicky.

Everyone else can burn in hell for all I care.

Skully finally calls me over and I pull my hoodie off, tossing it down next to Nicky before I do the same with my t-shirt. *Venom* by Eminem blares from the speakers set up on the ground near the fire, the sound mixing with the crack of thunder overhead. The eager crowd surrounds us on all sides and Skully hypes them up even more, not even bothering to state the rules before we start because there aren't any.

Whoever taps out or passes out first loses.

It's as simple as that.

Nicky sits with his elbows on his knees and his fingers linked together, his knuckles touching his lips while he watches my every move. Avery stalks towards me just as the first drop of rain hits my cheek, then Skully shouts *fight* and the crowd starts shouting, too, most of them high and hungry for blood. Instead of hanging back and waiting to see what I'll do first like most of them do, Avery rushes forward and tries to tackle me, the fucking idiot. Just as he reaches me, I catch him by his throat and toss him back like a rag doll, enjoying the shock on his face when his big ass hits the ground. I laugh to myself and shove my hands into the pockets of my sweats, damn near bouncing on my heels at the adrenaline coursing through me.

I fucking love this part.

He stands up to his feet and moves in to crowd my space, mouth open like he's about to say something mean, but he doesn't get the chance before I pull my arm back and punch him in the nose. He falls over again and I look at Nicky, doing a quick double take when I spot the new kid standing just a few feet behind him. He's leaning back against a tree with his arms crossed over his chest and a lit joint between his teeth, his creepy eyes zoned in on *my* little brother like he wants to eat him.

Over my dead body.

"… the fuck? *Kade.*"

I frown at the sound of Nicky's panicked voice, looking back at him just in time to watch him jump up to his feet. At first I can't figure out what's wrong with him, but then I feel the hand gripping my hair and the fist smashing into the side of my face.

This motherfucker.

Something hard hits my head and I blink a couple times, locking my jaw when I realize I'm on my back and Avery's on top of me, his weight crushing my chest and ribs as he punches me again. I lift my forearms up to protect my face and take a second to get my bearings back, then I grab the bastard by his shoulder and flip him over, straddling his waist with both hands wrapped around his throat. I cut off his airway and he kicks his legs out like a lunatic, his nails digging into my wrists as he tries to buck me off of him. His eyes widen with fear when he catches the look on my face, and I almost feel sorry for him.

Almost.

I should drag this out a little bit and make him suffer for that little stunt he pulled on me just now, but all I can think about is getting back to Nicky, which is why I release my grip on his throat and lay into him as hard as I can, over and over again until his body goes limp beneath me. My knuckles are on fire and my head is killing me, and I barely even register Skully calling me off before the boys are dragging me up to my feet, all three holding me back by my arms while I fight to get away from them.

"Dude, *enough!*" Mark shouts over the crowd, laughing like an idiot as he looks down at the guy passed out on the ground. "Goddamn."

I shove him away and stumble back a step, only relaxing when Nicky appears in front of me with his hands on both sides of my neck. His lips move but I can't hear what he's saying, and it's only now I feel the heavy rain pouring down around us. I'm soaked from head to toe, my arms and chest caked in a thick layer of dirt and a mixture of mine and Avery's blood.

"Kade?" he asks, bouncing his eyes between mine, his brows pinched with worry.

"It's nothing, Nicky," I mutter, turning my head to spit the blood from my mouth.

"It's not nothing," he argues, guiding me back to the log to grab my t-shirt. "I think you smacked your head on a rock when you went down. Why the fuck would you let him hit you like that?"

"It just happened," I lie, knowing the goddamn reason but refusing to admit it, fearing he'll *see* me for what I really am if I say too much out loud.

I'm fully aware my obsession with my own brother isn't normal or healthy, but I've been like this for years now and I can't seem to stop it.

Nicky, Nicky, Nicky.

He's all I fucking think about.

He presses my shirt to my temple and I grit my teeth at the sting, but I don't pull away. Instead I look down at him and let him do his thing, watching the way his eyes drop to the mess on my chest, then down to my abs and the waistband of my sweats.

I like his eyes on me like this.

I shouldn't, but I do.

His lips twitch like he knows it and he lifts his free hand to my mouth, carefully brushing his thumb over the bleeding cut there. Pushing his luck, he bumps his hips into mine and I almost groan at the contact, but then I remember where we are and snatch his waist with both hands. He makes a sound but I pretend not to hear it, discreetly telling him no with my eyes.

Not here.

He pouts a little bit and removes the shirt from my temple, his lean body crashing into me when fucking Jasper knocks into him from behind. I catch him before he falls and Jasper spins to face us, bravely reaching out to grab Nicky's upper arm.

"Shit, man, I'm sorr—"

"Back the fuck up," I growl, roughly shoving his ass with a single hand pressed to his chest.

He raises a brow at that, slowly stepping back with his hands up in mock surrender. He probably thinks I'm crazy, but I don't give a shit. I can't fucking stand this guy, and I swear to god if he winks at my little brother again I'll choke him right here.

"Dude," Nicky says, effectively pulling my attention back to him.

"What?"

"He said he was sorry."

"I don't give a fuck, Nicky." I snatch his jaw, forcing his eyes up to mine. "No one touches you."

"But you," he adds, playfully rolling his eyes when he catches the confusion on my face. "No one touches me but you, right?"

I look away and run my tongue over my teeth, glaring at nothing while his words run riot through my head.

Right.

"Can we go home now, please?"

I nod and release my grip on his face, taking my shirt from his hand to throw it on over my head. "Did Skully give you the cash already?"

"Yep," he says vaguely, laughing lightly when I turn my head to look at him.

"You gonna tell me how much?"

"Enough to buy me another hit for the ride back," he jokes, pulling the bills from his hoodie to slap them into my open palm. "Maybe one for yourself, too."

I snort at that, wrapping my arm around his neck to

scrub a hand through his hair. "Fucker."

"Jesus, will you keep still?" he complains, snatching my head when I try to pull it away. "I need to clean it."

"I already cleaned it in the shower."

"Well, you didn't do a very good job," he throws back, carefully dabbing the cut on my temple with a cotton ball soaked in something that burns.

I'm sitting on the fucking toilet seat wearing nothing but a towel around my waist, still high on adrenaline and restless thanks to the coke swimming around in my system. My knees are bouncing and my dick is refusing to stay soft and I'm fixing for him to leave so I can get myself off, but he's dead set on playing doctor and I'm the sucker who can't say no to him.

It's fucking maddening.

"Are you done?"

"Almost," he answers, moving down a bit to do the same thing with my lip.

I clench my teeth and look up at him, narrowing my eyes when I catch the amusement in his.

The little shit's enjoying this.

Ignoring my half assed anger, he tosses the dirty cotton ball on the counter and reaches over to grab a clean one, then he swings one leg over my thighs and drops his ass down on my lap, fucking *straddling* me like it's the most natural thing in the world.

Maybe it used to be, but that was *before*.

Everything after that night is brand new territory for

us and I'm fucking terrified of screwing it all up.

"Nicky—"

"It'll be quicker if I can actually reach you," he cuts in, holding the back of my head to keep me still while he finishes cleaning my lip.

My pulse hammers against the side of my neck and I fist my hands at my sides, resisting the carnal urge to grab his ass and *pull* until he's grinding on me.

You're sick, Kade.

So fucking sick.

As soon as he's done, he lifts my chin and leans in even closer, eyes on my mouth while he blows on it to ease the sting. A choked out noise slips from my throat and I flex my fingers, unsure whether I'm about to throttle him or force him to do it again. Before I have the chance to make up my mind, he chews his lip and looks down between us, then he takes my wrist and lifts it up to his mouth, staring right at me while he spits into the palm of my hand.

Jesus fucking Christ.

He climbs off my lap and I look up at him, watching him with my mouth parted while he collects his trash and walks out to my bedroom. He closes the door behind him and I blink, stupidly staring down at the small pool of my baby brother's saliva. Instead of washing it off like a sane person would, I lean back and flick my towel open, groaning at the feel of my wet hand sliding over my dick, my fucked up imagination feeding me several images that have no business filling my fucking head.

"Oh, *fuck.*"

CHAPTER 7

NICKY

WE DON'T TALK about Friday night.

We don't even acknowledge the fact that he used my spit to get himself off, that I leaned back against the door between us and came all over my hand at the same time he did, that we lay in his bed afterwards and watched a few movies as if nothing ever happened.

Denial.

It's his favorite game and he plays it like his life depends on it.

Walking down the hall on Monday morning, I side-eye him and steal the coffee he's holding, jumping when he smacks my hand to stop me.

"Hey."

"You've got your own."

"Mine's all gone."

He sighs heavily and takes another sip, handing it over to let me have the rest. I grin and he shakes his head in annoyance, but I don't miss the teeny little smile there that tells me he doesn't mind sharing.

Mark catches up to us and squeezes Kade's shoulders from behind, still excited about all the money he won the other night thanks to my brother and his crazy temper. I zone out when he starts talking and sip my new coffee, rounding the corner to find Austin and Parker talking to Jasper next to his locker. I'm not sure if Jasper has any real friends yet, but even though those two boys look like sweethearts next to Kade and Mark, they're not the best friends for him to have.

They'd beat the shit out of him if they knew he prefers dick over pussy.

"How long have they been brothers?" he asks them, leaning his shoulder against the wall with his back to us.

"I don't know, since they were three or four, I think," Parker guesses. "Kade's dad adopted Nicky and Nicky's mom adopted Kade after they got married."

"So, they're just one big happy family, huh?" Jasper mutters, almost smiling to himself as he sips whatever's in that to-go cup he's holding.

"Not anymore." Austin shakes his head, distractedly looking down at the phone in his hands. "Their mom was attacked and killed in her own kitchen a few years ago. Their dad was at work and Kade and Nicky were asleep upstairs."

"Who killed her?"

"No one knows. They never caught him."

"For real?"

"Yeah, but I wouldn't get caught asking about it if I were you," Parker warns, making him frown.

"Why not?"

"Because Kade—"

Before he can finish, Austin jabs his elbow into his ribs and Parker grunts, quickly snapping his mouth shut when he realizes we're standing right beside him. An awkward silence follows and I chew the inside of my cheek, looking over to find Kade staring directly at Jasper. His face is void of any real emotion, but I don't miss the small tick in his jaw or the way he inches closer to me, so discreetly you'd have to be looking for it to see it.

I'm pretty sure Jasper *is* looking for it, though.

The second bell rings and he finally takes the hint, smiling to himself again while he turns around to head into the class he and I share together. As soon as the others walk away, Jasper winks at me over his shoulder and Kade reacts without thinking, glaring down at me when I jump in front of him to block his path. My chest bumps his and I cling to his hoodie at his hips, holding him back with as much strength as I can muster.

"Kade, stop it," I hiss, terrified he's about to get himself expelled and leave me here all by myself. "Please, just walk away."

His nostrils flare and he looks around, checking to make sure no one's lingering in the hall, then he wraps his big hand around my throat and pushes me back against the wall beside the door.

"Jesus, what are y—"

"Don't sit next to him," he orders, trapping me here with his hips and his eyes, his other arm propped up on the wall above my head.

"But that's my assigned seat," I argue, struggling not to *moan* with his hard body pressed right up against mine. "I can't just sit wherever I want, Kade."

"No, but you'll do it anyway," he informs me, leaning over to tease my ear with his mouth. "You'll do whatever I tell you to do. Won't you, baby brother?"

God fucking damn him.

I nod once and he releases his grip on me, stepping back to allow me to walk into my class. I take a breath and force myself to move, avoiding any and all eye contact while I make my way to the empty desk in the back corner by the window. Jasper looks up when I pass him, frowning when he realizes I'm not taking my usual seat, but he doesn't say anything about it. I drop my ass down and pull my notebook from my bag, peeking up through my lashes to find Kade leaning back against the door frame, smirking at me with his hands shoved into the pockets of his jeans, the fucker. Satisfied he's manipulated me into submission, he leaves to go to his own class, and that's when Jasper glances at me over his shoulder, hitting me with a knowing look that makes me nervous as hell.

Fuck, this guy.

Luckily for me, the teacher doesn't call me out for switching seats without permission or reason, but I'm still on edge for the entire hour, worried she's about to notice and tell me to move back to my own desk. She doesn't do that, but the lesson still drags on and on, the same way it always does when I'm away from Kade for too long. As soon as the bell finally rings, I stand up and shove my stuff back into my bag, tensing when Jasper appears in front of me and perches his ass on the edge of my desk.

"Hey."

"Hey," I mutter, rolling my eyes when he hits me with that stupid look again. "What?"

"What?" he asks, his tone laced with an innocence that doesn't suit him.

I cock my head and he chuckles, checking to make sure no one's listening this time before he turns back to me.

"Nothin', it's just… your brother's a little… *intense.*"

I laugh lightly at that, nodding as I sling my backpack over my shoulder. "Yeah, I know."

"Are you going to Austin's party on Saturday?"

"What?" I ask, pulling my head back at the sudden change of subject. "Why?"

"You know why," he teases, dragging his lip through his teeth as he drags his eyes over my form, blatantly checking me out in front of everyone in here.

I swallow my fear and grit my teeth at him, warning him with my eyes to keep his fucking mouth shut.

No one but me, Nicky.

"Look, man, whatever it is you think you know about me, you're wrong."

"Is that right?"

"I like girls," I whisper harshly, leaning in as I squeeze by him to ensure he hears me loud and clear. "If you're smart, you'll say the exact same thing."

"I'm not that smart," he jokes, snatching my forearm to pull me back to his chest. "I can make you feel *real* good, you know? All you have to do is let me."

I shake my head and take a step back, slapping his hand away when he tries to grab me again. Before he has the chance to say anything else, I turn around and all but run away to find my brother, jumping out of my skin when I run right into him in the hall. He gets one look at me and glares, his hands clutching my ribs as he bounces his vicious eyes between mine.

"What the fuck happened?"

CHAPTER 8

KADE

Today's a *bad day*.

That's what our mom used to call them before we knew what depression was. The ones when her body and mind just refused to work with her, when she'd do nothing but lie in bed all day, unable to keep that fake smile on her face or eat or even talk to us.

Nicky's like her, but whereas she had more bad days than good, especially towards the last few months of her life, he has more good days than bad.

Most of the time.

I'll take him to get help after we graduate if that's what he wants, but for now all I can do is watch him suffer and keep on hiding the razor blades.

As if sensing my eyes on the scars I can't see beneath his hoodie, he locks his jaw and pulls his sleeves down to his knuckles, leaning back beside me on the three seater couch we're sitting on. Austin's tiny living room is bursting with drunk people, most of them too fucked up to think straight by this point, the lights low, the loud music drowning out the sounds of their shouts and laughter.

"We don't have to be here, you know?" I ask again, hoping to get an actual sentence out of him this time, but he just stares at his lap and flicks his lighter to burn the joint he's smoking.

I sigh and run my hand through his hair, discreetly kissing his temple before I move to stand. I walk over to the kitchen and grab him a bottle of water from the fridge, shaking my head when I find Austin and Parker making out with a set of smoking hot twins on the other side of the room. Mark walks over and grabs himself a beer from the box on the counter, tipping his chin at Nicky while he uncaps it with his teeth.

"What's wrong with him?"

"None of your fuckin' business."

He snorts at that, nodding to himself as he takes a sip. "Yeah, well, I think the new kid wants to know, too."

I tense and look up, struggling not to react when I see Jasper standing at the bottom of the narrow staircase, once again staring at my brother like he's the hottest guy he's ever seen.

"Kid looks like a fucking fag," Mark sneers, not even bothering to mask his disgust toward gays.

That's the problem with this bullshit town.

If you're *not* homophobic, you're not normal.

"He's not a fag," I mutter, keeping my tone bored,

inwardly wishing I could shove my fist down his throat. "I heard he likes Arianna's pussy just fine."

"Is that why you can't stand the guy?"

I don't answer that, hoping he takes my silence as a yes and moves the fuck on. He can think whatever he wants about me as long as it keeps his thoughts away from Jasper and the way he keeps eye fucking the only person who matters to me.

I won't allow this guy to take Nicky down with him.

I'll kill a motherfucker before I let that happen.

Mark gets distracted by some girl I don't recognize and I relax a little bit, but my anger soon bubbles up again when I catch Nicky's eyes locked with Jasper's. My cocky little shit of a brother tilts his head to the side and blows a thick cloud of smoke out, slowly moving his gaze over his form and then back up to his face. He looks like he's considering something, and I want nothing more than to walk up behind him, rip his head back by his hair, pull his eyes up to mine and remind him who he fucking belongs to.

Fuck.

I growl quietly and rest my elbows on the counter, slowly dragging my hands over my face in an attempt to clear my messed up head. The sound of glass smashing nearby has my eyes popping open and I look up at Nicky—the same thing I always do at the first sign of trouble—but he's not sitting where he was thirty seconds ago. Ignoring the girl picking up the broken glass beside me, I grit my teeth and walk over to the living room, shaking my head in denial when I realize Jasper's nowhere to be seen, either.

No.

This is not fucking happening.

I'm just about to rush upstairs, assuming that's where they would have gone, but then I spot Nicky just as he slips out the back door, nervously chewing his lip while Jasper leads him out with a hand on his spine. Fucking seething, I react the only way I know how and follow them outside, my teeth almost *cracking* at the sound of Jasper's whispered voice at the end of the small yard.

"...so fucking sexy," he rasps, grinding on my brother against the six foot fence. "You ever done this before?"

"Kissed a guy?"

"Done *anything* with a guy."

"Y—I mean, no. No, but I don't... fuck, I don't know if I can do this, Jas. I can't—"

"Yes, you can," *Jas* assures him, eagerly shoving his hand down between them. "Just relax, man. I know you're a virgin. I'll go slow, I promise."

Nicky winces and I lose my mind, snatching the white haired little cunt by his jacket to toss him back against the fence. His eyes widen when he realizes who grabbed him and he curses, but before either of them can get a word in, I pull my fist back and punch him hard in the face. His ass slides to the ground and I punch him again, unsure whether I've broken his nose or not considering my heart is racing and my veins are on fire with a rage I can't control.

He fucking *kissed* him.

Grabbed his dick and was about to take his virginity

outside when it's freezing cold, right here in Austin's back yard where any fucker could see.

I should fucking *kill* him for that.

Nicky's voice rings out from beside me but I ignore him for now, crouching down in front of Jasper to take his bloody jaw between my fingers. "If anyone asks, I saw you looking at Arianna and I didn't like it. If you tell *anyone* about what just happened, I'll turn every single one of those gay hating boys in there against you and I won't think twice about it. And if you *ever* put hands on my little brother again, I will put you in the fucking ground, you stupid piece of shit."

"*Kade.*"

"Shut up, Nicky," I bite out, roughly shoving Jasper's head back against the fence.

The urge to kick him while he's down is there, but then Nicky's squeezing my wrist and pulling me away, his eyes filled with shame and… shit, that's fear.

I blow out a breath and wrap my hand around the back of his neck, digging my fingers into his flesh while I drag him towards the gate at the side of the house.

I know I'm being too harsh.

I *know* he can't help who he is or who he's attracted to, but *fuck*, what if someone had caught him back there?

What if *Mark* had caught him?

I can't even think about it.

We get to the truck and I open the passenger side door for him, freezing where I stand when I catch the thick tears leaking from his eyes.

"Fuck, baby, did he hurt you?" I whisper, crowding his space to run my thumbs over his cheeks.

He sniffs and pulls his brows in, staring at me for a long second, but then his expression morphs into anger and he shoves me back. "No, Kade, *you* hurt me," he chokes out, punching me in the chest when he realizes I'm not about to move. "What you just *did*… this is *exactly* why I wish I never told you about me. You're just like *them.*"

He hits me again and I bat his fists away, pushing him back against the truck with my hand wrapped around his throat. "I didn't punch him because he's gay, you idiot," I grit out, so close my lips are brushing his. "I punched him because you're *mine.*"

Silence follows and he swallows against my palm, staring up at me with his mouth parted, breathing heavily against my face. "I… what?"

Fuck.

Fuck, fuck, fuck.

He starts to say something else but I slap my free hand over his mouth, squeezing my eyes shut when I feel his hard dick mashed up against mine. He squirms beneath me and I tighten my grip to keep him still, dipping my head to press my mouth to my knuckles, lightly resting my forehead against his.

"Get in the truck, Nicky," I say quietly, warning him with my eyes not to fuck with me right now.

After a full five seconds of hesitation, he does as he's told and I glance at the house over my shoulder, constantly at war with myself because despite what I said just now, he's not mine.

He *can't* be mine.

I repeat that thought as I walk around to the driver's side, but even then, the fact remains the same.

Of course he's fucking mine.

CHAPTER 9

KADE

Seventeen years old…

Something's wrong.

I can tell by the way he's run the water in the bathroom four times in the last twenty minutes, almost as if he's washing his hands or brushing his teeth over and over again.

I know he hates sleeping in his own bed, but he's never up all night like this and he's making me nervous.

Five times.

Just as I'm about to get up, Arianna places her hand on my cheek and pulls my mouth back down to hers, frowning when I snatch my face away to stop her.

"What—"

Ignoring whatever she's about to ask me, I pull out of her pussy and throw the empty condom away, tucking my dick beneath the waistband of my boxers while I walk to the bathroom. I push the door open and Nicky jumps a fucking mile, cursing himself when he accidentally knocks the ceramic soap dispenser off the counter. It smashes on the floor by his feet and he looks down at it for a second, avoiding my eyes as he bends down to pick up the pieces.

"Leave it," I order, closing the door behind me to ensure Arianna can't see him or his scars.

He pulls his hand away but remains crouched down on the floor, wearing nothing but his underwear and a faded black t-shirt that looks like mine. I cock my head when he continues to stay there, still refusing to look at me, and it's only now I realize how hard he's shaking, his black hair sticking out in all directions like he's been trying to yank it right out of his scalp.

"You okay, Nicky?"

"Yeah," he says, but I'm not an idiot.

He's been acting like this a lot lately and I *know* he's hiding something from me, that he's *lying* to me about something for the first time in over fourteen years.

I don't like it.

Careful not to cut my feet on the glass, I pick him up by his waist and set him down on the counter, fingering the fabric of the huge shirt covering his ass and the tops of his thighs. "You been stealing my shit again?"

He laughs shyly and nods his head, but then his laugh turns into a gag and he drops his face to his hands, hiding from me again. My heart aches for him and I move in to stand between his legs, gently taking his wrists to wrap his arms around my neck.

"Talk to me, baby brother," I whisper, my lips

touching the spot between his eyebrows. "I can't fix it for you if you don't tell me what's wrong."

"You can't..." he trails off, still shaking like a leaf, shivering like he's cold. "I mean *I* can't... because... *fuck.*"

I frown and run my hands over his upper arms, then around to his back to keep him warm. "Nicky?"

"You'll never leave me, right?" he asks randomly, lifting his bright gray eyes up to mine. "You promised, remember? You said—"

"I know what I said," I cut in, quickly glancing at the door before looking back to him. "And I won't. It's me and you no matter what, you *know* that. So quit playin' with me and just tell me what you did, okay?"

"I didn't *do* anything," he mutters, scooting closer to me, reaching up to lock his arms around my head. "It's not like that, I just... I can hear you fucking her through the wall and it's—" He gags again, almost like it's physically impossible for him to get the words out. "Shit, there's something *wrong* with me, man. My head's all messed up and I think... I think..."

Oh, fuck.

"Wait, Nicky, please, don't say i—"

"I think I'm gay."

Silence.

It stretches between us and then I'm moving, dragging him out to his bedroom by his forearm, tossing him down on the bed to pace the floor in front of him.

"Fuck," I growl, angrily ripping my hands through my hair. "*Fuck*, Nicky, why would you *say* that? *Out loud* when you know Arianna's right fucking there on the other side of that wall. Are you out of your mind?"

"I'm sorry," he chokes out, lifting his heels up to hug his knees, rocking himself back and forth the way he used to when he was little. "I know it's bad but I can't help it, Kade. I've tried and *tried* to like girls but I can't stop thinking about boys. Ones who'll hold me down and fuck me the way you fuck her. It's driving me crazy."

Jesus Christ.

"I'm sorry," he says again, wincing when he catches the look on my face. "Do you hate me?"

I glare at that, making him frown, but then it hits him and he releases the breath he was holding, dropping his head to rest it on his forearms over his knees.

He knows I could never hate him, gay or not, no matter what, I'll love him until the day I die.

"Dad, though…" he mumbles, peeking up at me when I say nothing. "He's gonna kill me, isn't he?"

"No."

"Kade—"

"I said *no*," I bite out, leaning over him to take his jaw between my fingers. "He won't kill you because you won't tell him. I don't care how desperate you get or how badly you need to be *fucked*. You won't tell *anyone* about this, you hear me? No one but me."

He nods the best he can with his face trapped in my grip, scooting back a bit to make room for me.

"No one but me, Nicky," I repeat, kneeling up on the bed to stalk towards him on my knees. "Say it."

"No one but you," he whispers, fear gone and

replaced with something I'd rather not think about.

Releasing his jaw, I lie down beside him and wrap my arm around his waist, grabbing the blanket to pull it over the both of us. He fidgets a little bit and then rests his head on my shoulder, chewing the inside of his cheek as he walks two fingers over my chest.

I've known about him for a while now, noticed the way he's never given a fuck about girls or pussy, seen the way he stares at my abs or my dick when he thinks I'm not looking, but I'd always hoped he wouldn't figure it out before we leave next summer.

Or ever.

That might make me a selfish piece of shit, but I've seen first hand what happens to gay guys in this town and I'm fucking terrified someone'll try to do the same thing to Nicky.

That constant fear of him getting hurt, whether it be here or someplace else… it's the bitch that keeps me up at night.

"What's wrong?" I ask after a while, tilting his chin up when he doesn't answer right away. "Nicky, tell me."

He rolls his eyes and drops his head back on my arm, hesitating before he decides to do as he's told. "It's stupid but I just… I really hate my life sometimes."

"What do you mean?"

"I mean you have your girlfriend and the boys and the entire school at your feet and what do I have?" he asks, laughing lightly like he thinks he's pathetic. "Mom's gone, Dad's a fucking lunatic, all my friends are *your* friends, and I can't even date anyone because I'm not allowed to like who I like. I have no one, Kade."

Fuck, is he serious?

"Look at me right fucking now," I demand, pulling his hair a little harder than I intended to, making him wince, but I don't stop until his eyes hit mine. "I don't give a fuck about any of those people and neither do you. You have *me*, baby brother. *I'm* your someone."

"But one day—"

"One day *nothing*," I stress, already knowing what he's thinking without having to hear it.

He thinks I'll marry some chick in ten years and live with her and have kids with her or some shit, and even though there's a chance that might happen—although it's a really fucking small one—I'd never even *think* about leaving him alone to live my life without him.

Nicky *is* my life and he *always* will be.

It's that fucking simple.

He stares at me and I stare at him, unsure what to say or where we go from here.

I don't tell him that he could find himself a boyfriend after we leave this town because I don't like that idea.

The thought of anyone touching him, of anyone *taking* him from me like that... it makes me fucking vicious.

Before I can think of a way to kill a fucker who doesn't even exist on my radar yet, Nicky grins like he's a mind reader and I blink, only just realizing my fingers are tangled in his hair and my mouth is less than an inch from his, our hard dicks pressed together through the fabric of our underwear.

"I love you, too, brother," he jokes, raising a brow when my cock jerks against his.

Fuck.

I should let him go—I *really* need to let him go—but I don't do that. I'm too focused on the way he's *still fucking grinning*, eyes on mine with his bottom lip trapped between his teeth. I glare at him but he pretends not to notice, lifting the blanket over our heads to cloud us in darkness. Twisting himself from my grip on his hair, he leans up on one elbow and runs his thumb over the corner of my lip. My mouth parts on its own and he kisses that same spot, shifting his body a little bit like he's trying to get even closer to me. He can't *get* any closer considering there's not a breath of space left between us, but it seems he's dead set on trying. He does it again and I snatch his waist to stop him, but then he sucks in a breath and his hips buck, causing his dick to rub right up against mine.

"Kade," he rasps over my lips. "Do that again."

"What? This?" I ask, digging my fingers into his waist.

His head falls back and he moans—fucking *moans* for me—grinding his needy little dick against mine as if he can't help but chase the friction. I must be out of my mind, because instead of pushing him away, I find myself taking advantage and dipping my head to taste him, lightly kissing the edge of his mouth the same way he did to me. He shivers and I drag his thigh up to my waist, rolling him over until he's flat on his back and I'm on top of him. I don't know what the fuck's gotten into us or who moves first, but we're full on kissing now and I'm letting it happen. I'm *kissing* Nicky, ignoring the fact that my girlfriend's waiting for me to make her come in the next room over, ignoring *everything* but the way his soft lips feel moving against mine.

Fucking perfect.

Needing to feel more of him, I rake my fingers through his hair and pull, stretching the collar at his neck to taste the pulsing vein there. He moans again and I lick him slowly, freezing when a distant knock fills my ears, followed by the sound of Arianna's tired voice.

"Kade?" she calls, knocking again when she gets no answer. "Babe, you still in there?"

My shoulders lock and I pull back a bit to look at Nicky, fucking horrified when I realize what we were just doing, what *I* was just doing to my own brother. He clings to me but I shake my head no, grabbing his wrists to pin them to the sheet either side of him.

"That didn't happen."

"Kade."

"That didn't happen, Nicky," I hiss, pushing myself up to toss the blanket away. "Jesus."

His face crumples with rejection and I leave before I do something stupid, like retake that empty spot between his thighs and fuck his mouth with my tongue, dry fuck him and make him moan again until he comes all over himself.

Fucking stop.

Shaking those disgusting images from my head, I lean my hands on the bathroom counter and cringe at my own reflection, barely able to look myself in the eye because *fuck*.

What the fuck have I done?

CHAPTER 10

NICKY

HE CALLED ME HIS.

He called me *his* and I can't stop thinking about it.

The way he choked me tonight and shoved me back against the truck, the way he *claimed* me like that…

It was fucking hot.

But now he's avoiding me.

Not physically but mentally, keeping his back to me while he runs a towel over his wet hair, refusing to look at me as he pulls his sweats on and grabs the cigarettes from his nightstand. He lights one up and leans his shoulder against the wall next to the window, deep in thought as he looks down at the quiet street we grew up on.

I know he doesn't like whatever this *thing* is building between us, but I'm desperate for his attention and I won't stop until I get it back.

Sighing heavily to ensure he hears me, I push myself up from the edge of his bed and walk over to stand behind him, sliding my hands over his ribs to wrap my arms around his waist. He tenses and I close my eyes, breathing him in while I move my fingertips over the dips and ridges of his abs.

"Are you mad at me, Kade?"

"No," he answers, blowing his smoke out the window.

"Okay, then," I mumble against his spine, inching my fingers down to trace the lines of the deep vee just above his waistband.

"I'm not mad at you, Nicky." He takes my hands, moving them back up to safer territory. "I'm just mad."

"About what?"

He doesn't answer that, just like I knew he wouldn't because he's a stubborn asshole. I roll my eyes and reach up to steal the cigarette from his mouth, turning him around to sit him down on the window seat. He finally looks at me and I take a hit, slowly lifting my thighs up one at a time to straddle his hips.

"Is it because of Jas?" I ask, smirking when I catch the tick in his jaw. "Is it because he would have turned me around and fucked me right there against that fence if you hadn't shown up when you did?"

"Nicky…" he warns, but I'm feeling reckless and drunk and so fucking horny I can't think straight.

"Is it because you can't stop getting hard for me?" I tease, holding on to his shoulders to move in closer, bravely rolling my hips on his dick. "I bet that's it."

He glares like he wants to choke me again, but then he takes my waist with both hands and *squeezes*, causing a moan to slip from my throat before I can catch it.

He did that on purpose.

I shiver and wrap my arms around his neck, careful not to burn him with the cigarette I'm still holding, dipping my head until my mouth touches his. "I know you want me," I whisper, sliding my tongue over the fading cut on his bottom lip, enjoying the way his cock thickens even more between my legs. "You want me now… you wanted me the night you kissed me…" I go on, grinding on him a little harder this time. "I think you've wanted me since before I told you I was gay."

"Fuck, Nicky, *stop,*" he rasps, effortlessly picking me up to drop me down on my feet, walking away from me to light himself another cigarette. "We can't do this."

"Why not?"

"Because you're my *brother*, you sick fuck."

"Stepbrother," I mutter, as if that makes it any better, but he just laughs and shakes his head at me.

"That's bullshit and you know it. Get the fuck out."

"Kade."

"I said get out!" he shouts, making me jump.

My mouth parts and I back away from him, my eyes stinging with the effort it's taking not to cry because in all the years I've been pushing my luck to get a rise out of him, he's never yelled at me like that.

Never.

Not missing the look on my face, he curses and takes a step towards me. "Nicky, wait—"

But I just keep on walking and slam his bedroom door behind me, not looking back when I hear a smash against the wall a few seconds later.

"*Fuck.*"

CHAPTER 11

KADE

I've thought it a thousand times over in the last twenty nine hours, lying awake and alone in my bed because Nicky straight up refused to come back to me. Aside from mandatory church with Dad and Elle yesterday morning, he locked himself up in his room for the rest of the weekend and only came out to eat once. I glared at him when he grabbed the cereal bar from the kitchen cupboard last night, told him to sit his ass down and wait for me to cook him a proper fucking meal, but he just looked right through me and took a bite out of it, barely acknowledging my existence before he walked back upstairs to hide from me again.

We've fought a few times over the years, mostly over stupid shit like brothers do, but never like this.

I hurt him this time and it's making me sick.

After I don't know how many hours of staring at the ceiling, my alarm finally goes off and I hit the stop button, forcing myself up to get ready for school. I shower and brush my teeth in what feels like slow motion, then I wrap a towel around my waist and try the door between the bathroom and Nicky's room, not really surprised to find it locked, the same way it's been locked since he left me two nights ago.

Since you yelled at him and kicked him out, you prick.

"Nicky," I call, sighing when he doesn't answer. "Nicky, come on, don't make me kick the fuckin—"

The door suddenly opens and I shut my mouth, pulling my brows in while I move my gaze over his form. He looks more exhausted than I am, black hair a fucking mess, his eyes bloodshot and *empty.*

"Did you sleep at all last night?" I ask, but he just moves around me and grabs his toothbrush from the sink, holding himself up with his free hand on the counter as if it's taking all his strength not to fall over.

The urge to grab him is there and I almost do it, almost snatch his waist and pull his back to my chest, desperate to *feel* him and force him to talk to me, but I can't. I *can't* because every time I touch him like that, every time I've got my hands on his body and his ass on my dick, I want him in all the ways I shouldn't.

He was right before.

I want him and I can't fucking *have* him.

It's making me crazy.

When I do nothing but stand behind him and stare at his reflection, he looks up at me and side-eyes the door, working his jaw a little bit when I make no move to leave. "Do you mind?" he mutters, the words muffled by the toothbrush hanging from his mouth.

Words.

They're not very good ones, but words are progress.

"I'll go warm the truck up," I tell him, not missing the small flash of disappointment on his face before he dips his head to spit.

Don't touch him, Kade.

Not in here.

I'll make him talk to me on the way to school, when he's wearing more than just his underwear and I have a little more sense of self control.

With that being the best and only plan I have, I leave the bathroom and grab a clean pair of jeans from my closet, shaking my head at myself when I spot the smashed up lamp sitting in the corner.

Self control.

Right.

I DON'T FEEL LIKE EATING THIS MORNING, SO IT'S NO surprise Nicky doesn't, either. Hair still wet from his shower, he bypasses the kitchen completely, typing on his phone while he pulls his black hood over his head. He walks to the front door and I follow him outside, scrubbing a hand over my face when he doesn't even look back to check if I'm coming. Determined to fix what I broke, I move for the truck and open the driver's side door, looking over when I hear two cars pulling up on the road behind us. The first one's our dad, only just getting home from work, but the second car is one I recognize from school, the same one that belongs to Jasper fucking Whyte. With two black eyes and a nasty cut on his nose, he looks right at me and I snap my head to Nicky, my nostrils flaring when he continues walking *past* the truck with his eyes on the ground, his hands shoved into the front pocket of his hoodie.

He wouldn't dare.

It seems he would, though, because before I can even think about stopping him, he slides into the passenger seat and shuts the door, his shoulders pulled up to his ears as he mutters something I can't hear.

Drive.

He told him to drive.

"Who the hell is that?" my dad asks, but I'm already gone, all *self control* forgotten while I watch them disappear around the corner.

A fucking dead boy is what he is.

I PULL UP IN MY SPOT NEXT TO MARK AND RIP MY BAG from the passenger seat, ignoring the boys standing around outside as I make my way across the parking lot. I'm pretty sure everyone's staring at me like I've lost my damn mind, and maybe I finally have, but not one of them moves to talk to me or get in my way.

They *know* not to get in my way.

Unlike this fucking guy who doesn't seem to get that I *will* kill him if he doesn't back the fuck off of what belongs to me.

I get to his car and yank Nicky out by his elbow,

making him stumble, dragging him with me while I walk around to the driver's side.

"Kade, chill, it was just a ride," Jasper chuckles, climbing out with his hands raised either side of him, smirking to himself as he side-eyes Nicky over my shoulder. "It's not my fault he chose me over y—"

"Listen here, you little cunt," I cut in, stepping closer until my chest bumps his, arms behind my back as Nicky pulls on my wrists from behind. "I won't tell you again. Stay the fuck away from my brother."

"Or what?"

A laugh bubbles out of me and I shake my head at him, deliberately moving my eyes over his messed up face. "You don't wanna know."

He grins and rolls his eyes like he thinks I'm adorable, seemingly unbothered by the fact I'm *this* close to kicking his ass twice in two days. Knowing I'll do it, Nicky pulls me a little harder this time and I force myself to go with him, turning around and pushing him back just to crowd his space again.

"Move."

"*No*," he says clearly, and I know he means it, but I'm too fucking mad to listen to reason right now.

Mad, I can deal with.

Mad gives me a solid excuse to put my hands on him, to grab the little brat by his hoodie and take him with me, to hide him behind my truck and wrap my fingers around his tiny little throat.

So that's exactly what I do.

His breathing picks up and he takes a hold of my wrist, cursing when his back hits the passenger side door. The first bell rings but I ignore it, leaning over him to steal his phone, my fingers shaking with rage while I delete Jasper's number, then block it.

"Don't *ever* get in a car with a guy who's not me."

"Why not?" he asks, half bored, half mocking. "Because I'm *yours*? You really gonna say that to me right here where any fucker could hear you?"

I keep my mouth shut and he nods, hitting me with a look that says *yeah, I didn't think so.* I glare at him and study his annoyingly perfect features, dipping my head to brush his nose with the tip of mine. He remains deadly still for a few seconds, but then he shivers and I move across to his cheek, enjoying the way he still melts at my touch even when he's pissed at me.

"What do you see in that guy, Nicky?" I whisper, sliding his phone back into his front pocket, keeping my hand there to graze his abs with my knuckles. "Why did you go with him?"

"He's my friend."

"Yeah?" I taunt, dragging my thumb over the column of his throat, making him swallow. "Does your *friend* know you're only using him to torture me?"

"I don't think he cares," he answers, not even bothering to deny it. "He just wants to fuck me."

"Is that what you want?"

"You know what I want, brother," he says simply, bravely tipping his head back to look me dead in the eye. "But if you won't give it to me, it's nice to know I can get laid someplace else anytime I need it."

"You little bitch," I grit out, roughly digging my fingers into his jaw, but he just laughs humorlessly and shoves me back, purposely looking me up and down as he takes a slow step away from me.

"Yeah, well… I'd rather be a bitch than a pussy."

LATER THAT NIGHT, I FIND MYSELF LEANING MY SHOULDER against the door between my bedroom and the bathroom, listening to him like a creepy stalker would while he brushes his teeth before bed.

He sat next to me in every class today, ate five bites of the lunch I put in front of him and got in the truck after school without issue, but he still went right back to ignoring me after I pinned him in the parking lot, wouldn't even look at me unless it was to hit me with that painfully blank stare he seems to have mastered overnight.

The fucking silent treatment.

I'd rather let him punch me in the face a hundred times.

He's doing everything he can to stay away from me and I don't really blame him for it, but I'm not about to let him spend another night without me, either.

I'm done with this shit.

As soon as I hear him unlock the door on my side of the bathroom, I fling it open and walk inside to grab him from behind, completely disregarding my *no touching* rule to lock my arm around his waist. He squeals and looks at me over his shoulder, relaxing when he sees it's me, but that relief doesn't last very long.

"Get off me, Kade," he growls, kicking his legs out when he realizes what I'm doing. "Jesus, are you crazy?"

I ignore that and carry him to his room to grab his phone from the nightstand, then I take him back to my bed and toss him down on it. He tries to get up but I'm faster, pinning him down with a single hand on his bare abs. He stares at me in shock and I plug his phone in to charge, carefully climbing over his body to take my spot beside him. He huffs out a breath but doesn't bother to argue, and when I roll him over to his side and yank his back to my chest, I swear I can *hear* him smiling into his pillow.

He likes me crazy.

I pull the blanket over us and tangle my legs with his, linking our fingers together on his chest to hold him tight against me. It only takes him five minutes to fall asleep, if that, and as soon as I know he's out, I'm right there with him, finally allowing myself to relax for the first time in days.

CHAPTER 12

KADE

THE GUY I'm fighting taps his hands on the ground and I remove my arm from around his neck, dropping his head to push myself off of him. Wincing at the probable pain rushing through his skull, he rolls over onto his back and covers his face with his forearms, his chest heaving with the effort it's taking to breathe again. I leave him there and walk to the edge of the circle, glaring at the boys around me when I feel their hands on my shoulders. They back off a bit and I look at Nicky, slowly moving my gaze over his form while he takes the cash from Skully's hand. He's wearing all black tonight, his dark hair messed up the way he likes it, his fingers subconsciously rubbing his face over and over again, probably because I haven't shaved him in a few weeks.

I should do that soon.

Just as I think it, our eyes lock and he chews the corner of his lip, looking down to shove the screwed up bills into his pocket. I sigh and take a seat on the log in front of me, still watching his every move while I grab the pre rolled joint he left me on my hoodie.

I hate this fucking wall between us now.

I hate the fact that he makes me want to tear it down and pull him into my arms.

And I hate myself for these stupid thoughts that won't leave me the fuck alone.

I just want us to go back to the way we were before.

Before I yelled at him just for wanting what I want, too, before I lost my shit and called him *mine*, before I kissed him that night under the covers, before I started thinking about him in a way no guy should think about another guy, let alone his own fucking brother.

Goddamnit.

"You know, I've been thinking about it, and I think I've figured it out," Jasper says, dropping his ass down beside me despite the fact I didn't tell him he could.

My jaw ticks at his continuous bravery but I keep my eyes forward, resting my elbows on my knees to burn the end of my joint. The creepy little shit irritates me so much that I've fantasized about choking him until he stops breathing, but still, I can't help but take the bait.

"Figured what out?"

"The reason everyone's so blind when it comes to you and Nicky," he explains, scooting closer to me, half flicking his wrist towards the large group of teenagers we've known for most of our lives. "You've been brothers since before kindergarten, right? So they've watched you grow slowly. They only see you as brothers who love and look out for each other because that's all you were when they met you. They don't notice the way you're crazy about each other because it's been happening for years, little by little, so subtle you can't see it unless you're looking."

By the time he's finished, my shoulders are tense and my hands are itching to close around his throat, but I refuse to look away from Nicky. He's watching us with his eyebrows dipped in confusion, his eyes fixed on the way Jasper's body is way too close to mine, the clear doubt there causing my fingers to curl around the lighter in my hand.

He's jealous, and I could beat his ass for it.

He should *know* I would never.

Because even though my cock wants nothing more than to be buried inside him, I'm not gay.

I can't explain it, but it's only ever been him.

No one but him.

"Jesus Christ," Jasper mutters to himself, shaking his head at us in amusement. "Do you want my advice?"

"What I *want* is to kill you with m—"

"If you don't hurry up and take what's right in front of you, someone else is gonna take it first," he says simply, laughing at me again when he catches the look on my face. "Relax, you psycho, I didn't mean me. Nicky doesn't want me like that and I'm not desperate enough to keep trying. I'm just sayin'… your little brother looks hot tonight. Imagine what he's gonna look like in two years or five," he adds, widening his eyes to emphasise his point. "They're gonna want him bad, Kade."

I cock my head at that, leaning in a little further until

his face is just a few inches from mine. "Get the fuck away from me."

He smirks at the venom in my tone and pushes himself up to his feet, casually walking away like he doesn't have a care in the world. Nicky comes over to stand in front of me and I look up at his face, inwardly seething over Jasper's bullshit words.

I don't like what he said, but I'm not blind, either.

Nicky's equal parts beautiful and sexy. Both awkward and cocky. Innocent and dirty. A nerdy little freak wrapped up in a body that was made to be held down and fucked.

"Kade…"

Of course they'll fucking *want* him.

My hands are shaking just thinking about it.

"Kade," he repeats, frowning when I don't answer right away. "What the hell did he say to you?"

"Nothing."

"But—"

"You ready to go?" I ask, standing up to grab my shit.

He hesitates but nods, not so discreetly staring at my abs as I pull my jacket on over my shoulders, not bothering with my shirt.

"Yeah," he says. "Okay."

I leave it unzipped and take a couple long hits of my joint, passing it to him while I blow my smoke out to the side. I tilt my head at him and he falls in line beside me, rolling his eyes when he spots Arianna sulking with her group of friends by the campfire, eyes narrowed on us as she watches us leave. I'm sure she still thinks we're together or some shit, but she's not stupid enough to walk right up and ask me to take her home.

If I wanted her pussy tonight, I'd go and get it.

She knows that.

"Aren't you gonna talk to her?" Nicky mutters, although it's clear he doesn't like that idea.

"Talk to who?" I ask, shoving my hand into my back pocket to grab the keys for the truck, grinning to myself when I feel his eyes on the side of my face.

He doesn't say anything right away, but I don't miss the way he dips his head to hide his own grin. "No one."

***

As soon as I've showered and washed the dirt from my body, I dress in a gray pair of sweats and grab the box of razor blades I keep stashed on the top shelf of my closet, too high for Nicky to reach without help.

It's not that I don't trust him, but we talked about it the last time I caught him cutting himself and he agreed that it was better this way, not just for him but for both of us.

I take a clean one out and put the box back, then I walk through to his bedroom and open the door, thankful he quit locking me out after I dragged him back to my room last weekend. He's been sleeping in my bed every night since, but I know he's still a little put out over what happened between us. I can tell by the way he's acting, waiting for me in here instead of in my room, not coming to me as soon as the fight ended tonight, not asking me to shave him like he usually does when he wants it done…

He's distancing himself from me on purpose, almost like he's afraid I'll reject him again if he comes too close. And even though I'm too chicken to call him out on it, it's killing me on the inside.

I *miss* him even though he's right fucking there.

Less than ten feet away from me, he's sitting back against his headboard with his knees up and his head-phones in his ears, once again touching his face while he watches something on his phone. I'm assuming he's not getting himself off under his sweats considering his hands are nowhere near his dick, but I don't miss the way he jumps and hides his phone in his lap when he catches me standing here.

"What are you doing?" I ask, cocking my head at him while I twist the razor in my hand.

"Nothing," he lies, smiling shyly when he realizes what I'm holding. "What are *you* doing?"

I smile back and crook my finger at him, hiding a laugh when he jumps up like his ass is on fire, hot on my heels like he's worried I'll change my mind if he's not fast enough. He hops up to sit on the bathroom counter and I fill the sink with warm water, tipping my chin at the hoodie he's wearing.

"Take that off."

He wiggles his arm out and pulls it up, but then his eyes widen and he stops, dipping his head to hide the heat creeping over his face. I frown and open the cabinet beneath us, doing a quick double take at him when my head goes someplace I wish it wouldn't.

"Take it off," I repeat slowly, straightening up to stand between his legs, placing my hands on the counter either side of him to ensure he can't get away.

He looks embarrassed, but not ashamed or afraid like he'd be if he was hiding fresh cuts from me.

Knowing I won't drop this, he takes the hoodie off and I scan the pale flesh on his arms, instantly relieved when I realize it's not what I thought it was. Still blushing like a nun, he averts his eyes and wraps his arms around himself to hide the t-shirt he's wearing— *my* t-shirt—lightly kicking my thigh when he catches the amusement on my face.

"Shut up," he mutters, making me laugh for real this time. "You're such an asshole."

"I didn't say anything."

"But you're thinking a lot of things," he throws back, frowning when I fist the hem of the shirt to pull it up over his abs. "Hey—"

"I'm not taking it," I assure him, clutching the fabric at his ribs. "You can have it back after, okay?"

He nods and allows me to pull it the rest of the way off, chewing his lip while I lean over to grab the shaving cream. I stand between his legs again and squeeze a bit into my palm, gently moving his chin up to spread it out over his face. He doesn't have many hairs besides the few at the corners of his mouth, maybe a couple tiny ones on his cheeks and his chin, but he still insists on me shaving his whole face the way I do mine.

I dip the razor into the water and hold the back of his head, keeping him as still as possible as I drag the blade over his skin, carefully and slowly to ensure I don't cut him. He remains quiet and watches my face the entire time, his eyes moving between mine and my mouth, almost like he can't decide where to look.

"Why didn't you ask me to do this for you?" I ask, tipping his head back to shave the edge of his jaw.

He shrugs a little bit and I grit my teeth, warning him with my eyes not to fucking move like that again. He rolls his lips and I fist his hair, stretching his neck a little more to drag the blade over his throat. As soon as I'm finished, I toss the razor into the sink and wipe the excess cream with a warm washcloth, gently dabbing a towel over his face to dry him off. A few drops of water slide over his chest and I dry those, too, enjoying the way his mouth parts with my hands on his body.

"What were you watching before?"

He blinks at that, but then he leans back and raises a brow, easily reading my mind the way he's been able to since we were kids. "Why do you keep asking me questions you already know the answers to?"

Because I'm an idiot.

"Nicky."

He cocks his head and stares at me for a long second, highly amused by whatever he sees there. "Porn."

"What kind of porn?" I force out, working my jaw when he raises that cocky little eyebrow again. "Tell me."

"Gay porn, brother," he says simply. "You know… boys kissing boys, eating each other with their tongues, fucking each other in the as—"

I glare and wrap my right hand around his throat, using the other one to tangle my fingers through the hair at the back of his head. "What the fuck have I told you about that?" I hiss, forcing his eyes up to mine. "If you forget to clear your history and Dad goes through your phone…" I trail off, letting that awful sentence hang in the small amount of air between us. "I told you not to watch it anymore."

"But I can't help it, Kade," he whines, reaching down to squeeze his cock over his sweats, visibly shivering at the feel of his own hand. "It's so fucking hot."

"Are you trying to piss me off?"

"Yes," he admits, scooting closer to wrap his arm around my neck, still playing with his dick between his open legs. "But only because you want me to. Because even though I might pick fights to get attention, I think *you* pick fights to be close to me."

"Yeah?"

"Yeah," he echoes, his warm breath ghosting the side of my face. "Is this enough?"

I lean over him and shake my head, squeezing my eyes shut as I fight the urge to do something I shouldn't, something wrong and disgusting and dirty. "More."

"I was looking for a threesome video," he whispers in my ear, lightly trailing his fingertips over my neck. "I wanted to picture you fucking my ass and Jasper fucking my mouth at the same tim—oh, shit, *Kade*!" he squeals, laughing when I pick him up and throw him back against the wall beside the door, my hips pinning his with his legs wrapped around my waist.

He smirks and I glare, roughly digging my fingers into his thighs, secretly enjoying the way I can *see* his pulse hammering against the side of his neck.

"Is this what you wanted?" he rasps, holding himself up with his forearms around my shoulders.

I let out a breath and nod my head, shaking it just as quickly because *no*, I don't *want* this.

I don't *want* to want him this way.

I don't *want* to feel this rage inside me every time I think about someone else taking what's mine.

I don't *want* to feel any of this but I can't fucking stop it.

"I can't stop it, Nicky," I confess, dipping my head to breathe the air from his mouth. "I *can't*."

"Stop trying, then," he pleads, desperately squirming against me, punching my arms when I do nothing but stare at his lips. "Damn it, Kade, you have to stop playing with me like this. *Please*. Either kiss me right the fuck now or let me walk away."

But I can't let him walk away—not *right the fuck now*, at least—and if those are my only two options…

He punches me again and I let him do it, once, twice, three times… then I lose my fucking mind and smash my mouth on his. He jumps and I grab the back of his neck, tilting his head to the side for better access, eagerly moving my lips against his soft ones.

So fucking soft.

As soon as the initial shock wears off, he opens up for me and I lick his tongue, making him moan.

"Holy shit," he gasps into my mouth, writhing between me and the wall. "Holy shit."

"You said that already."

He lets out a shaky laugh and runs his hands over

my chest, then down to the waistband of my sweats, frowning when I snatch his wrists to stop him.

"No."

"What?"

"You said you wanted a kiss," I remind him, dragging his bottom lip out between my teeth. "Don't touch."

He sighs impatiently and I pull his jaw down with my thumb, gritting my teeth when he does it again not five seconds later.

"I just told you not to touch me," I growl, pinning his hands to the wall either side of his head, linking our fingers together to ensure he can't move.

"Fuck, Kade, please," he begs. "I want it so bad."

"My cock?"

He nods like a crazy person, dropping his forehead on mine to look down between us, his own dick hard as a rock and trapped against my abs.

"Tell me where," I demand, digging my nails into his knuckles. "Where do you want it?"

"In my mouth."

I mutter a curse and he manages to rip his hands from my grip, pushing me back a step to drop to his knees in front of me. He spreads his legs out like a porn star and curls his fingers over my waistband, grinning up at me with his tongue trapped between his teeth, the little demon. I've officially lost it by this point and I don't think I've ever been this horny, which is why I allow him to pull my sweats and boxers down and kick them the rest of the way off, grunting when he squeezes my hips and takes me into his mouth without hesitation.

"Jesus, fuck," I choke out, holding on to the back of his head, placing my free hand on the wall in front of me to keep myself steady. "Fucking hell, Nicky."

He mumbles something I don't catch and moves up and down on my dick, spitting on it and stroking my length with the flat of his tongue. I know he's never done this before, but you wouldn't think it by the way he's gagging and choking himself without issue. He looks fucking beautiful down there, his eyes watering thanks to the lack of air in his lungs, his pouty lips stretched out around the base of my cock… it's enough to drive me bat shit crazy.

"Nicky," I whisper his name, unsure where I was even going with that. "Jesus…"

He makes a sound and carries on sucking me, driving me *wild*, looking awfully pleased with himself when he catches the look of helplessness on my face. Because even though he's the one on his knees right now, he's got all the power here and he knows it.

He licks the tip and I groan, pushing his head back to gain access to his throat. He squeezes my outer thighs and I consider that consent, slowly rolling my hips out to fuck the wet heat of his mouth. It seems he doesn't want it slow, though, because then the little slut digs his nails into my flesh and forces me in even further. I bang my fist against the wall but give him what he wants, tightening my grip on him to fuck him a little faster, deeper and *deeper* until my pelvis is pushed right up against his nose. He gags again and I hold him there, releasing him after a couple short seconds to let him catch his breath.

"Is that good?" he rasps, pulling off to rub his spit over my dick. "Tell me I'm good, Kade."

"You *are* good, baby," I assure him, not forgetting the look he gave me when I called him that outside Austin's house last weekend.

It slipped out by accident that first time, but I like the way his pretty eyes light up when I say it.

He grins up at me and I grin back, bending over him to wipe the tears streaming over his cheeks with my thumbs. I kiss him and lift him up to his feet, shaking my head when he opens his mouth to argue.

"I don't wanna come yet," I explain, making him frown.

"Kade, that was barely five minutes."

I tilt my head and he stares at me in confusion, but then it hits him and he smirks, running his hands over my wrists to keep himself steady, standing up on his tiptoes to kiss me back. I tighten my grip on his face and back him up into my room, kicking the door shut behind me before I walk him over to my bed. The backs of his knees hit the mattress and he sits down on it, his eyes flashing with heat and hunger as he moves them all over my body. I fist my cock and he licks his lips, moving forward like he's about to taste it again. I push him away from me and shove him down on his back, using my knees to nudge him up towards the headboard.

"One night," I whisper, leaning over him to kiss the edge of his jaw. "You gonna be okay with that tomorrow?"

He nods and tips his head back on the pillows, but I don't think he's really listening to me.

"I mean it, Nicky," I stress, pulling back an inch to look at him. "This is only happening *once*. Never again."

He nods some more and opens his legs for me, boldly grabbing my head to pull my mouth down to his neck. Knowing what he wants, I lick his pulse and dip my hand beneath his waistband, groaning when I realize how much his cock is leaking already, soaking my fingers and the inside of his boxers.

"Fuck, you weren't lying, were you?" I breathe out, slowly moving my palm over the underside. "You want it *that* bad? You're fucking *wet* for me?"

He whimpers at that, lifting his ass off the bed to push himself into my hand. All this useless fabric between us is getting in the way, so I sit back on my heels and pull the rest of his clothes off, tossing them to the floor before lying over him again. He kisses me and I tangle our tongues together, fucking loving the way his naked body feels spread out under mine, my bare cock grazing his hole with every grind of our hips. I wrap my hand around him and jerk him off slowly, rocking into him hit for hit, struggling to breathe properly because *fuck.*

Fuck.

"This is so fucking wrong," I point out, but my stupid dick won't stop dry fucking my little brother's ass.

"I like wrong," he says lazily. "Wrong feels good."

"Fucking brat."

He chuckles and bites my lip, but then I bite him

back and he chokes on his own air, moaning for me when I squeeze the head of his cock.

"God. *Kade.*"

"What, baby?" I taunt, manipulating the shit out of his body and mind, using my left hand to run my nails over his scalp. "You want me to make you come?"

"Yeah."

"Yeah?"

"Damn it, Kade, stop fucking teasing m—"

I bite him harder this time and let go of his dick, sliding two fingers through the precum there before moving them down between his legs. Shifting to line my cock up with his, I watch his face while I rub his hole, enjoying the way he reacts to that one simple touch. His eyes slam shut and he opens his mouth, his hips bucking wildly against mine.

"Oh, fuck."

"You like it?" I ask, nudging his thighs with my knees to spread him out a little more.

"Yes."

"More?"

"*Fuck*, yes."

I give him what he wants and slide the tip of my finger inside him, still grinding on his hot little body, and fuck me, the sounds I'm drawing from his throat…

Just as I think it, he cries out loudly and I slap a hand over his mouth, because even though the walls aren't *that* thin, I can't risk the neighbors telling our dad they heard him screaming my name up here.

He mumbles a string of curse words against my palm and I look down, my eyes darkening at the sight of his cock pulsing between us, his hot cum shooting out all over our dicks and abs, his tight ass squeezing the fuck out of my finger. That sets me off and I come before I can stop it, removing the hand from his mouth to replace it with my tongue, shoving it inside to shut us both up. My hips flex by themselves and he clings to me, wrapping his hands around my neck and his legs around my waist.

"Fuck, Nicky," I whisper against his lips. "You okay?"

"Yeah," he whispers back, dropping his head with a goofy ass grin that makes me want to *kiss* him all over again.

Jesus.

How the fuck did we get here?

I know I've done him wrong and the guilt is there, but I don't feel sick about it like I thought I would.

Instead I feel… I don't know, *happy* or some shit.

It's fucking weird.

Nicky frowns at the look on my face and I shake my head no, gently running my hand through his hair while I kiss his cheeks and his eyelids, then down to his jaw and across to his earlobe.

"It's not you, baby brother," I tell him, which sounds cliché as fuck, but it's the truth. "You're perfect."

As soon as he relaxes again, I lie down beside him and pull him into my arms for a while, not so patiently waiting for that *need* to disappear now that I've had him the way I've wanted him for years.

It doesn't disappear.

CHAPTER 13

NICKY

I SMILE to myself and run my thumb over the scar on the inside of his left hand, struggling to think about anything but all the dirty things he did to me last night, all the dirty things he let *me* do to *him*…

It was fucking amazing.

I don't know what he's gonna think when he wakes up with a clearer head, but I honestly don't care about that right now. I feel happier than I've ever been after what we did, and I'm fully fine living in this state of naivety, even if it's just for a little while.

I'm lying on my side with his arm wrapped around my back, wearing the huge t-shirt he put me back into after we washed the cum from our bodies last night, my hips pushed up against his with my leg locked over his lap. I trace his scar again and he slowly nudges my thumb with his, touching *my* scar, then he links our fingers together and guides our hands up to his bare chest.

"Why are you awake, Nicky?" he asks, the sound muffled by the pillow we're sharing.

"I can't sleep."

He pops his eyes open at that, staring at me with something that looks a lot like panic, probably worried he's scarred me for life or some shit. "Are you—"

"Horny," I tell him, rolling my hips out a bit to let him feel my hard on. "It won't go away."

He laughs lightly and kisses the spot where my jaw meets my ear, his other hand moving down to the base of my spine. "Are you hungry?"

"Yeah," I croak out, but we both know it's not for food.

I want his dick in my mouth again.

I want to kneel on the bed between his legs and drive him *crazy*, let him rip my hair out and fuck my skull until my throat burns for days afterward.

Just as I move to touch his waistband, he takes my hand again and holds it up between our mouths, kissing each knuckle before doing the same with my fingertips. My jaw ticks and I rest my head on the pillow, still facing him head on with our noses touching, silently cursing myself for agreeing to his stupid *one night* rule so easily.

I should've persuaded him to give me two while I had him on his metaphorical knees.

We lie like that for I don't know how long, in our own little bubble where nothing and no one else can touch us, and for the first time in a long time, he allows me to really *see* him. The way his chest aches behind that heartless mean boy mask he wears all the time, his dark eyebrows pulled together like he's in pain, his bright blue eyes telling me things his mouth never will.

Because no matter how much we want it, we can never be together like that, and I think it kills him just as much as it kills me.

"Do you love me, Kade?" I whisper, unable to say it any louder without choking.

"Always."

"Even if I love you too much?"

He smiles sadly and moves the hair from my eyes, leaning in a little closer to brush his lips against mine. "We have to get up now, baby brother."

And just like that, he's telling me it's over.

It's *over* before it even started.

I swallow the lump in my throat and force myself to move away from him, avoiding his eyes while I sit up on the edge of his bed. I hear him stand behind me and pull my heels up to my ass, dropping my face to my hands to dig my palms into my eye sockets.

He told me I had to be okay with it and I am.

I *am*, goddamn it, but it still fucking hurts.

Pulling my own mask into place, I take a deep breath and stand up to grab the cigarettes from his nightstand, side-eyeing him when I feel him staring at my legs, his shirt so long on me that it looks like I'm not wearing any underwear beneath it.

He's playing a dangerous game looking at me like that, but I don't think he even realizes he's doing it.

"Kade."

He blinks and clears his throat, leaning over to grab his clothes off the floor. "Put some pants on."

"Why?" I ask, smirking a little bit when he hits me with a look that says *shut your fucking mouth or I'll shut it for you.* "I'll put pants on if you leave that off," I counter, tipping my chin at the shirt in his hands.

He raises a brow and drops his eyes to his abs, the sexy bastard, then he looks up and moves towards me, slowly twisting the fabric he's holding between his fists. Knowing he's about to whip my ass, I turn around and make a run for it, squeaking out a laugh when he chases me around the bed. I rip his bedroom door open and run out into the hall, grunting when I smash right into a hard chest. I bounce back and Kade catches me with his arms wrapped around my waist, his entire body tensing against mine when he realizes what stopped me.

"Shit, s-sorry, Dad," I stammer, lifting my shoulders up to my ears when I catch the look on his face.

He's supposed to be on his way to Vermont for Elle's birthday weekend, told us he was picking her up from her house right after work this morning and driving up there straight away. I'd have never left Kade's room looking like this if I knew he was here.

He's here.

Fuck.

Fuck, what if he'd have walked in on us just now?

The thought makes me sick to my stomach.

He moves his eyes over my outfit and sneers, flexing his hand like he's about to hit me for it, but then Kade spins me out of the way and steps closer to him, his chest bumping Dad's when he continues to come for me.

"Don't you fucking dare," Kade growls, roughly shoving him back by his shoulders.

Dad shoves him just as hard and I scrape a fingernail over my wrist, struggling to ignore the inner demon that begs me to *cut, cut, cut.*

I just need to let it out.

It hates me as much as I hate myself and I need it—

"Nicky, *stop.*"

I jump and look up at Kade, discreetly hiding my arms behind my back when I notice Dad's attention on my scars. I'm sure he already knows they're there, but he's never looked twice or tried to confront me about it. He doesn't *believe* in mental health issues, same way he doesn't believe in the act of being gay. He was just as indifferent with our mom and her depression, and I'd be stupid to believe he'd cut me any type of slack for mine.

Bouncing his evil eyes between me and my protector, he laughs cruelly and lifts his hands up in mock defeat. But we all know if this was three years ago, Kade would be on the floor by now and Dad would be on top of him.

"Elle left her bracelet here," he says by way of explanation, looking directly at me as he moves for the bedroom across the hall. "Take that off and wear your own fucking clothes, you scrawny little pussy."

I flinch before I can stop it and Kade closes his eyes for a second, locking his jaw while he waits for him to leave us alone. As soon as he's gone, he turns to face me fully and takes my waist with both hands, backing me up into his room to shut the door behind us. I wrap my arms around his head and bury my face into the crook of his neck, not missing the way his pulse is hammering beneath my lips.

"I'm sorry," I whisper, but he just digs his fingers

into the shirt I'm wearing and holds me even tighter, keeping his back pressed against the door to ensure Dad can't get in here without breaking it down.

A few seconds go by and we listen for the footsteps in the hall, then on the stairs, relaxing as one when we hear the front door slamming with his exit.

"I hate him, Kade."

"I know, baby," he says quietly, lifting one of his hands to run it through my hair, clearly trying to distract me. "What do you wanna do tonight?"

"Nothing."

"No?" he asks, his mouth curling into a smile against my temple. "What if I take you to get fucked up at the cabin?"

I pull back at that, grinning at the thought of spending the night there with him. "Really?"

CHAPTER 14

NICKY

"Who the fuck invited her?" I mutter, half flicking my wrist at the kitchen window, leaning my elbows on the huge wooden island in the middle of the room.

"Mark, probably," Kade answers, keeping his back to me while he restocks the fridge with alcohol. "He told all the girls to come, Nicky. Not just her."

I make a noise and rest my cheek on my fist, feeling awfully sorry for myself while I watch Arianna and her friends climb out of the car outside.

I thought he meant we'd be alone when he asked me to come this morning, but then he called Skully to get us some drugs and Skully told Mark, then Mark told *everyone*. Now the cabin is full of people we go to school with, some already drunk and half naked in the ten person hot tub on the back deck.

This place used to belong to our mom's parents, and even though they kicked her out when she got pregnant with me—because having a baby out of wedlock was against their religion or whatever—it was still left to her when her mother died six years ago.

The house is a huge, two story building sitting at the bottom of a steep mountain covered in snow, right on the edge of the lake we used to swim in every summer. Our dad wouldn't let us come up here anymore after Mom was killed, so Kade stole his keys a couple years ago and had one cut for us while he was asleep. We don't use it much out of fear of getting caught, but Dad won't be back until Monday afternoon and there's no way he'll find out unless we tell him.

Arianna walks through the front door in a pair of six inch heels, wearing a white fluffy coat that makes her look like a snowball, and I look away, rolling my eyes when I catch Kade's amused ones on me.

"Why you in a mood?"

"I'm not in a mood," I lie, reaching for my beer on the counter in front of him, gritting my teeth when he takes it first and holds it hostage between his palms.

"No more until you eat something."

"Damn it, Kade, you're not the boss of me," I hiss, both hating and loving that stupid smirk on his face.

"Yes, I am," he points out, slowly dragging his teeth over his lip while he slides me the pizza he had delivered just now. "Eat."

I feign a glare and snatch the smallest piece from the box, taking a childish, exaggerated bite out of it. His eyes darken and I purposely lick the sauce from my finger, dipping my head to suck it into my mouth.

"Nicky…"

"You told me to eat, brother," I tease, moving along to do the same with the middle one. "I'm eating."

"You fuckin—"

"Yo, boys," Mark calls out, tipping his chin at us as he walks over with some random blonde girl under his arm. "Which one's your room?"

"Third door on the right," Kade says, straightening up a bit to pass me my drink. "Take any other one you want."

Mark grins and picks the girl up by her ass, enjoying the happy giggle she lets out as he carries her over to the stairs. I shake my head at him and face forward again, pulling my brows in when I find Jasper leaning back next to the sink, gesturing between me and Kade with a mixture of confusion and interest.

"You two are sharin' a room?" he asks, and Kade's jaw locks up, his hands curling into fists on the counter separating us.

"There's a couch in there, too, you little weirdo," Parker chuckles, walking over to scrub a rough hand over his head, easily distracted, it seems. "Did you dye your hair to get it this white, or what?"

"No, I was born like this," Jasper deadpans, hiding a laugh when Parker nods like he believes him.

"That's bad luck, man."

I snort and Jasper raises a brow at me, keeping his eyes on mine as he grabs himself a beer from the fridge, uncaps it with his teeth, and then *slowly* sucks a drop of stray liquid from his middle finger.

Fucking hell.

I don't know if I'm *that* obvious with my feelings for

Kade or whether he just watches us *that* closely, but neither of those possibilities are good ones.

This boy has trouble written all over him.

And even though I was kind of using him before to piss my brother off, I can't deny the guy makes me a little nervous, especially after I watched him talking to Kade about fuck knows what last night.

"Kade, baby, it's freezing in here," Arianna whines from beside me, wrapping that stupid coat around herself with an exaggerated shudder. "Can you throw some more wood on the fire, please?"

My teeth clench at the word *baby* and I look at Kade, finding him staring at me because he's been staring at me this whole time, our eyes locking for a couple seconds too long before he pushes himself off the counter. He goes with her and I glare at nothing, ignoring Jasper and everyone else while I tilt my head to light a cigarette. He's a persistent fucker, though, and ignoring him isn't as easy as it looks.

"You gettin' high tonight, sweetie?" he asks, leaning his elbows on the island next to me.

"What makes you think I'm not high already?" I throw back, not even bothering to acknowledge the nickname that makes me feel like a six year old kid.

He cocks his head and studies me for a second, his intense gaze moving all over me and my body. "Kade doesn't let you drink or do drugs on an empty stomach, and something tells me that was all you've eaten today," he adds, tilting his head at the pizza box.

I roll my eyes at that, grabbing a red cup from the

stack in front of him to flick my ash into it. "You really think you know it all, don't you?"

"I know enough," he says cryptically, stealing the cigarette from my mouth to take a hit.

He blows his smoke into my face and I'm just about to ask what the fuck his problem is, but then he looks at something behind me and laughs, passing the cigarette back before slowly backing away.

"Calm your ass down, man. I'm leaving."

"Leave faster," Kade grits out, placing both hands on the back of my chair, his knuckles gently grazing my back through my hoodie, a direct contrast to his tone.

As soon as Jasper's gone, he leans over my shoulder and grabs a bottle of tequila from the island, discreetly pressing his mouth to my ear as he takes the salt and limes. "You gonna sit here and sulk all night?"

"I'm not *sulking.*"

"Of course not, baby brother," he taunts me, his hot breath causing a shiver to run down my spine.

"I hate you."

"You little liar," he whispers, glancing around to check no one's looking, then he pulls my head back by my hair and motions for me to open my mouth.

I stick my tongue out to show him my throat and he feeds me a little pink pill, gently brushing his thumb over my bottom lip as he watches me swallow it dry.

"Good boy," he praises, releasing his grip on my hair to tilt his head toward the living room.

I smile to myself and move to follow him, sidestepping my way through the crowd as we make our way to the boys by the coffee table in the middle. Someone turns the music up and everyone starts doing shots, snorting lines off the girls' bodies and watching them dance by the fireplace. Minutes turn to hours and I suddenly feel high as fuck, my mood significantly better than it was when I first got here.

I don't know where Kade is, but I do know he's watching me from somewhere, because he never takes his eyes off me when we party like this. I'm just about to go look for him, but then some girl appears in front of me and blocks my path. Her lips are painted black to match her long, shiny hair, and the black eyeliner she's wearing makes her eyes look really big and blue.

"You're cute," she shouts over the music, placing her wrist on my shoulder to move in a little closer.

"Um… thank you," I say lamely, staring at her pretty eyes for I don't know how long, then dropping my stare to her chest. "You're… not wearing a shirt."

She laughs like she thinks I'm the sweetest thing she's ever seen, wrapping both arms around my neck to roll her hips into mine. Her pierced nipples brush my chest and I panic, gently taking her shoulders to hold her mouth away from my face. Without offering any type of explanation, I smile politely and turn around to get the fuck out of there, my cheeks heating when Austin snorts and shakes his head at me. I'm sure everyone thinks I'm too much of an awkward loser to get laid, but the thought of hooking up with a girl makes my dick soft, and I'd rather let them say what they want about me than put myself through that shit again.

I kissed a girl once and it did not end well.

Still a little flustered over what just happened, I walk to the kitchen and grab a bottle of vodka from the side, cursing when I stumble over the step I forgot was there. I fall into someone's arms and look up, grinning when I realize it's my sexy older brother.

"You found me."

"I never lost you," he says back, holding my hips to keep me steady. "You ready for bed?"

I nod lazily and drop my face to his chest, lifting the vodka up over my head to show it to him. "Can I take this with me?" I slur, snorting when he snatches it and sets it down on the counter. "You're such a daddy."

"Nicky."

"A really mean one," I go on, slowly trailing my fingertips over his abs through his shirt. "And hot, too."

"Jesus, will you shut up?"

I chuckle and wrap my arm around his neck, fucking loving the way his warm body feels against the side of mine. He holds me up with one arm around my waist and walks me to the stairs, his jaw ticking a little bit when we pass Austin dancing with the black haired girl who tried to kiss me just now. At first I think Kade's mad at him for something, but then I realize he's glaring at the back of *her* head, not his.

"What are you smiling at?" Kade mutters, but I just hide my face and smile some more, purposely dragging my feet until we get to the top of the stairs.

Once we reach the bedroom we used to share in secret when we were younger, he opens the door and turns me to face him fully, backing me up towards the bed with my head cradled in his hand.

"You can stop faking now," he whispers in my ear, fisting my hoodie and shirt to pull them up over my stomach, his knuckles brushing the oversensitive flesh there.

I grin again and look up from beneath my lashes, enjoying the way he still wants to help me get undressed when he knows I'm fully capable of doing it myself. Wanting that, too, I lift my arms over my head and he pulls them the rest of the way off, tossing them down on the floor before tracing the waistband of my jeans with his thumb. My hips buck and he bites his lip to hide a laugh, popping the button with ease to push them down over my ass.

"Lie down," he orders, and I happily obey, kicking my shoes off before dropping back against the pillows.

He pulls my jeans and socks off and drops them on the pile, then he leans over me and kisses my jaw, passing me the unopened bottle of water he must have grabbed from downstairs without me seeing.

"Stay here," he says quietly, pressing another kiss to the other side of my face. "I'll be back soon, okay?"

I frown at that, pulling my head back to look at him properly. "What? Where the fuck are you going?"

He stares at me and I let out a scoff, petulantly tossing his stupid water bottle on the floor.

"Nic—"

"No, *fuck you*, Kade," I bite out, sighing through my teeth when I catch the internal struggle in his eyes, fisting my cock through my boxers to show him what he's done to me. "Why did you just do that? *Why* do you keep torturing me like this?"

"I'm torturing myself, too, Nicky," he admits, looking down between us to watch me get myself off, the muscles in his arms tightening at the sight of me.

"Stop it, then," I rasp. "Stop hurting us."

"I *can't*," he stresses, snatching my wrists to pin them to the pillow over my head, lowering his face to graze my open mouth with his. "Fuck, baby, I wish I could."

I whimper and seek his body out with my hips, squeezing my eyes shut when he pulls back a bit to stop me. "Kade… please, don't fuck her."

"I'll be back soon," he repeats, more decisive this time, pushing himself off of me to walk away.

The door slams with his exit and I punch the sheet, lifting my hands up to scrub them over my face, disgusted by the images of him and Arianna running rampant through my head. A few long minutes go by and I let out a humorless laugh, sitting up a bit to fist my dick again, spreading my legs to take it out fully.

"Fuckin' asshole."

I'm so fucking mad at him for leaving me like this, but I'm also fucked up on whatever was in that pill he gave me, horny as fuck and desperate for something to fill my ass. I lean over the bed and unzip my bag to search for the lube I stashed at the bottom, jumping when the bedroom door swings open behind me. I whip my head over my shoulder and find Kade pacing the room, angrily ripping his hands through his messed up hair. I frown and prop myself up on my elbows, confused as to why he's back so soon, and why he looks so mad at himself.

Is it because he fucked her… or because he *didn't*?

"Did you…?"

He shakes his head and suddenly stops pacing, slowly moving his dark blue eyes over my bare dick, then back up to my face. I grin like a brat and he glares, still pissed, it seems, but I don't think I've ever seen him this hungry, either. That's a dangerous combination in Kade, but I'm too far gone to care. I want him and I've *got* him, whether he likes it or not.

"Two nights," we say together, and he nods, closing the distance between us to claim my mouth with his.

I fall down on my back and wrap my hands around his neck, digging my heels into his ass to encourage him to grind on me. He does and I moan at the feel of him, eagerly running my fingers through his hair to chase his tongue with mine. He slides a hand over my throat and chokes me with it, then he curses into my mouth and pushes himself back up to stand.

"Kade, I swear to god," I growl, convinced he's about to leave me again, but he just smirks at me over his shoulder and pushes the wooden dresser in front of the door, blocking it to ensure no one can get in here.

Pulling his shirt over his head, he walks back over to me and pushes his zipper down, probably to give his dick some breathing room, taking a little bag of white powder from his pocket to toss it down beside me.

"You swear to god *what*?" he taunts, kneeling up on the bed between my thighs, pulling a note from his wallet to roll it up. "What will you do to me, baby brother?"

I open my mouth but snap it shut just as quickly, too busy thinking about all the things I *really* want to do to him, staring at his ridiculously hot body while he grabs the cocaine and spreads a line out on my abs. He uses a card to neaten it up and then dips his head to my stomach, lifting the note to suck the drugs up through his nose. I shiver and he slides his tongue over that same spot, cleaning me up, crawling over me again to bump my nose with his. Knowing what he wants, I open my mouth and lick it off of his tongue, tangling his and mine together to ensure I get it all. Without breaking the dirty kiss, I reach down and take the note from his hand, but he just shakes his head and snatches it back, throwing it down on the nightstand beside us.

"Hey—"

"That's all you're getting," he informs me, running his big hand over my inner thigh.

"But—"

He digs his fingers in and I whimper, closing my legs around him to fight the overwhelming sensation, but of course he doesn't allow that.

"I said that's all you're getting," he repeats, pushing my thighs out even further this time, spreading me wide open for him.

"Why do you always get more than me?"

"Because I'm bigger than you," he teases, looking down between us to examine the length of my body. "God, you're so fucking sexy."

I smile shyly and he kisses my neck, moving across to my throat and down to my chest, touching and *squeezing* every inch of my flesh he can get his hands on. I make a needy little noise and he licks my nipple, making me jolt, my eyes rolling back in my head at the feel of his mouth on me there.

"You like that?"

I nod and he does it again, using his tongue and his teeth to drive me insane. My hips fuck his pelvis and he rocks into me, using his free hand to push his jeans and boxers down over his cock, using our combined precum to rub it against mine.

"Oh, fuck," I rasp, awkwardly wiggling my toes into his waistband. "Kade."

He takes the hint and pulls back to get them all the way off, quickly pulling my boxers down and over my legs while he's at it. As soon as we're both fully naked, he pins my thighs to the sheet with both hands and fucks me without fucking me, dipping his head to bite and suck my lips into his mouth. My heart races and I dig my nails into his waist for leverage, secretly enjoying the way he seems to have lost his fucking mind.

I love how hard he gets when he's high, how vicious and desperate he gets for a hole to fill, how his pupils blow up until his eyes are almost black with need.

Needing him just as much, I reach out and feel around for the lube I dropped on the bed before, boldly shoving it into his hand once I find it. He blinks at that, turning it over in confusion, but he doesn't bother to ask me where I got it from. Knowing what I want from him, he uncaps the bottle and squeezes some out onto his fingers, moving them down between my legs to rub my virgin hole. I suck in a breath and he slides one inside me, slowly fucking me with the tip the same way he did last night. I hold on to his hair and he carefully pushes it in a little further, still nipping my lips while he grinds his cock against my inner thigh.

"I need more, Kade," I plead. "Fuck."

He smirks and gives me what I asked for, adjusting his angle to finger me even harder. By the time he's managed to slip a second one inside me, I'm shaking beneath him and squeezing the life out of my dick, desperate to make this last as long as possible.

"How hard do you wanna come right now?" he asks, running his tongue over the seam of my lips.

"Shut the fuck up," I grit out. "Asshole."

"What?"

"Nothing."

He raises a brow and bats my hand away, twisting his fingers to stretch me out, then he reaches for his own dick and slides it between my ass cheeks.

Oh, fuck, yes.

He rubs the tip over the edge of my hole and I lift my hips up for him, fisting the sheet with both hands when he does nothing but tease me with it.

"Goddamnit, Kade, put it in."

He freezes at that, lifting his eyes up to bounce them between my crazy ones. "Nicky…"

"*Kade.*"

"Fuck, I *can't*, baby," he chokes out. "This is enough."

"It's *not* enough."

"I know," he admits, dropping his forehead on mine, breathing heavily against my lips. "I know but it *has* to be. I can't fuck you, Nicky. You're my little brother."

"I won't tell anyone."

"I'll hurt you."

"I can take it," I promise him, pushing his face back to look him dead in the eye. "Please, Kade. I don't want to give it to anyone else. I want it to be you."

He groans like he's being tortured and I grin on the inside, knowing he can't say no to me when I beg him like that. He glares at the look on my face but snatches the lube all the same, cursing me to hell and back while he covers his cock with it. He pours what feels like half the bottle on my ass and then tosses it aside, scooting forward on his knees to line himself up with my hole.

"If it's too much, you tell me to stop, okay?"

"Okay," I agree, and he leans over to kiss me, trapping my leaking cock between our abs.

"Tell me again."

"I want you," I rush out, lifting my hips up to try and get him in. "Please. I want you so fucking b—"

He finally gives me what I've been dying for and I cry out into his mouth, squeezing my eyes shut while I wrap my arms around his neck. He feels fucking *huge*, but I'm pretty sure that's only the tip considering our bodies are still a few inches apart.

I force myself to keep breathing and he rewards me with his tongue, waiting for me to calm down before he slides it in a little more. Just as he starts to move, I bear down on him the same way I do when I fuck myself with my fingers, pulling him all the way in until his hips are pushed right up against my ass.

"Oh, fuck."

"Jesus Christ," he growls, his voice strained like it's

taking everything he has not to fuck me into the mattress. "Jesus fucking *Christ*, you little shit."

"You said that already," I manage to say, feeling so full, so stretched out that I can barely breathe.

A light laugh leaves him and he runs his hand over my ribs, nudging my face to nip the shell of my ear. "You gonna be quiet for me?" he asks, and I shake my head no, unable to stop the noises leaving my throat.

He reaches over and grabs his phone from the pocket of his discarded jeans, somehow keeping his dick in my ass while he connects it to the wireless speaker we brought with us. *Blood // Water* by grandson fills the room and he sets the speaker on the nightstand, turning the volume up to ensure no one'll hear me. Eyes on mine, he leans up on one elbow beside my head and licks my lips, coaxing my mouth open to tease my tongue with his.

"Mine," he says simply, and I swear to god I almost cry.

I bear down on him again and he grinds on me, fucking me slowly at first, then a little harder, pinning me down by my throat as he rubs my dick with his pelvis. It still hurts a little bit, but the way he fills me feels so fucking good, so fucking *right* that it's easy for me to forget the pain.

I wrap my hands around his wrist and dig my fingers in, wordlessly begging him not to stop, curling my toes into the sheet to fuck him back hit for hit.

"Jesus, Nicky," he rasps, looking down between us to watch our hips move. "You like being fucked?"

I nod and keep going, desperate to please him,

snatching his face to pull his mouth back to mine. "I told you I could take it. I'm taking it all, Kade."

"I know you are, baby," he says softly, moving his thumb down to slide it over the edge of my hole, his eyes darkening to black as he rubs it better for me. "You take it so fucking good."

His praise makes me weak and he takes full advantage, stealing my wrists to hold them down above my head, running his free hand over my abs to jerk me off. He adjusts his angle slightly and I let out a scream, my mouth falling wide open at the feel of him inside me.

"Is that it?"

"*Fuck*! Yeah, that's—oh, *shit*," I moan, curling my back to keep him right there. "*Kade.*"

Thank fuck he knows what I'm trying to say, because I can't string a sentence together to save my life. Still hitting that same spot, he fucks me even harder and I scream some more, shaking and pleading while he forces me to come all over myself. We groan together and he stills deep inside of me, squeezing the last of the cum from my dick as he fills me up with his own.

Fucking fuck me, that feels good.

As soon as he's done, he falls down on me and wraps both arms around my back, trapping me beneath him with no way to escape. "You good, baby brother?"

I nod and smile against his cheek, enjoying the way he can't seem to keep his hands off me even after he's fucked my ass raw. We stay like that for a long time, with his mouth on my neck and my fingers in his hair, unable to hear much besides the music blaring from the speaker next to us. Just as I think it, he reaches over to press the stop button and slowly pulls his dick out of my abused hole, leaning over the bed to grab the cigarettes from his jeans. I sit up a little bit and he sits back beside me, pulling the blanket over our laps before he tilts his head to light one. We pass it back and forth and I side eye him every few seconds, not missing the tick in his jaw as he stares at the wall in front of us.

"What's wrong?" I ask after a while, suddenly feeling a little self conscious. "Was that not—"

"It doesn't work."

"What?"

"It doesn't fucking *work*, Nicky," he hisses, standing up to snatch his jeans from the floor, then he moves for the bathroom in the corner and swings the door open.

He pulls a towel from the rack and I cock my head to the side, rolling my lips to hide a laugh when I hear the bath water running a few seconds later.

"Quit laughing at me and get your ass in here," he shouts, making me laugh for real this time.

Moody bastard.

CHAPTER 15

KADE

WAKING up without Nicky wrapped up in my arms has me jumping out of bed like it burned me, that constant pit in my stomach growing even more intense the longer he's without me.

Alone…

Unprotected…

Fuck.

I shove a clean pair of sweats over my legs and damn near fall down the stairs, frowning when I realize how clean the cabin is. It should be a mess after the party we threw last night, but the entire place looks exactly the same as it did when we got here yesterday.

What…?

Just then, Nicky's quiet voice fills my ears and I follow the sound, stopping in the open archway when I find him singing to himself at the kitchen sink. He's drying the dishes with my headphones in, lightly bopping his head to whatever song he's listening to on my phone. I can't make it out because he can't sing for shit, but I can't help the way my lips twitch while I watch him, either.

He looks happier today, probably because everyone else seems to have disappeared and we're finally alone. I know he wanted it to be just the two of us up here, but I couldn't tell Mark *no, man, you can't come with me because I'm taking my baby brother away for a romantic weekend in the mountains so I can get him high and steal his virginity.*

Jesus Christ, I took his *virginity* last night.

I thought having people around would help me keep my hands off him and my dick *out* of his ass, but it turns out I'm still a sick fuck no matter who's in my way.

Still singing to himself, he doesn't spot me as he continues cleaning, standing up on the very tips of his toes to put a glass away in the top cabinet. He's too short to get it up there without climbing on the counter, but that doesn't stop him from trying. I lean my shoulder against the brick wall and stare at his ass, shaking my head at him when he grits his teeth in frustration. Without thinking too much into it, I walk over and press my bare chest to his back, effortlessly taking the glass from his hand to place it on the shelf for him. He hides a grin and pulls the buds from his ears, tipping his head back on my shoulder to look at me.

"Show off," he teases, chewing his lip as he bounces his eyes between mine. "You look mad."

"Yeah, well, I was ready to choke the shit out of you about three minutes ago," I mutter, sliding my hands beneath his hoodie to run them over his abs.

He shivers and I check the doorway, dipping my

head to kiss the crook of his neck, enjoying the way he moans for me when I'm barely even scratching the surface.

"Where is everyone?"

"I kicked them out."

"Did you?" I ask, amused by him and his blatant lie.

"Fine, I didn't kick them out. They all left for church, but I *did* lock the door after them all by myself."

I laugh lightly and squeeze his waist, leaning over him to slide my tongue from his throat to his ear. "That's two days in a row you've been up before me," I point out. "You got somethin' on your mind, baby brother?"

"Just you," he answers, taking my hands to move them down a little lower. "I can't stop thinking about you."

"What about me?"

"The way you kiss me," he whispers, arching his back out to push his ass into my dick. "The way you touch me like this. The way you fucked me so hard I can still feel you now. I want you to do it again."

I groan at that, pulling his head back by his hair to shove my tongue into his mouth. He whimpers and I dip my fingers beneath his waistband, slowly running my hand over his cock through his boxers. He's already hard and leaking for me, just like I knew he'd be, and just like that, I'm losing my goddamn mind all over again.

Fuck, what is *wrong* with me?

But even as I think it, I know exactly what's wrong with me.

It's *him*.

Nicky's my kryptonite, and I was stupid to convince myself having him once would be enough.

One night... two nights... fucking *fifty* nights wouldn't take away this animalistic need I have to show him who he belongs to.

He's mine and I need him to know it, to *feel* it the way I feel it every minute of every goddamn day.

With that task in mind, I squeeze his dick and he moans into my mouth, still grinding his ass against my sweats. "Oh, god."

"I know, baby," I say softly, using my left hand to push his waistband down to his thighs, brushing my middle finger over the spot I filled just a few hours ago. "Does it hurt?"

He shakes his head and I smirk, knowing he'll say just about anything to get me to sink my cock into this needy little hole. I won't, because I really did fuck him hard last night, but I can't stop myself from picturing the way he'd look bent over the kitchen table with my fingers around his throat, the wood bruising the front of his thighs while I own him from behind.

No, Kade.

Taking my own cock out, I slide it between his ass cheeks and get him off at the same time, pulling him back against me to encourage him to keep moving.

"Good boy," I rasp, kicking his ankles out to get the angle I want. "Fuck my hand and make yourself come."

He whines and lifts his arms up, wrapping them around my head to hold onto my hair. I groan at the pressure and sink my teeth into his neck as payback. He cries out and I run my hand up to his chest, pinching his nipple between my thumb and forefinger.

"Harder, baby."

He curses but does as he's told, rolling his hips out even faster, his mouth falling open as he chases his own release. After a few more seconds, his dick pulses in my hand and he comes, shaking in my arms while he makes a big mess on the counter in front of us. I pull his mouth up to mine and kiss him again, sucking his tongue into my mouth, fucking loving the way his bare ass feels sliding up and down on the underside of my cock.

"Tell me you'll fuck me again," he demands, and I fucking come all over his hole, nodding my agreement while I rock against him to ride it out.

"I'll fuck you again."

He smiles and I sink to the floor, bringing him with me to pull him into my lap. Unbothered by the cum dripping between his thighs, he lifts his knees up and rests his head on my shoulder, gently running his clean hand over my throat and chest. I kiss his temple and wrap him up in my arms, not so patiently waiting for my heart rate to return to normal. It takes a long time, but this weird feeling swirling around in my stomach doesn't seem to be going away any time soon, especially not when I'm with him.

Jesus, what *is* that?

"What did you mean last night, Kade?" he asks quietly, avoiding my eyes as he draws an invisible picture on my ribs. "When you said it doesn't work. What doesn't work?"

"I thought I could fuck you out of my system," I say honestly, not surprised when he tenses against me.

"What?"

"Like when I'm fucking Arianna," I explain, tightening my grip on him to rest my chin on the top of his head. "As soon as I come I'm ready to kick her out on her ass. That doesn't happen with you."

"No?"

"Not even a little bit," I admit, taking his hand from my hip to lock my fingers with his. "Every time I'm with you I just *want* you more and more, over and over and over again. It feels… weird. And annoying. And confusing."

"I don't think it's confusing," he argues, still hiding from me, and I don't have to see him to know he's smiling again. "I think it means you're in love with me."

I frown at that, pulling my head back to look down at him. "Why do you make it sound so sweet?"

"What's wrong with that?"

"My love for you isn't sweet, Nicky…" I lift his chin up with my forefinger, picturing all the bad things I'd do for him to keep him safe, all the things I'd make *him* do for me to protect my sanity. Like forcing him to switch seats to keep him away from Jasper. "It's toxic."

But he just shrugs his little shoulders, shifting his body to press his lips to mine. "I'll take it either way."

Once I've gotten some breakfast into him at Lucky's Diner, I drive him home and pull up on the street outside the house, holding my door open for him so he can jump down from the driver's side. I grab our bags from the back seat and follow him inside, dropping them by the front door to lock it behind me.

"Does this mean I'm your boyfriend now?" he asks randomly, lifting his straw to suck on the strawberry milkshake he brought home with him.

I blink and scrunch my nose up, openly staring at him in disgust. "The fuck, Nicky?"

"Well, I just thought…" he trails off, his face falling as he glances between me and the small window. "That was a date, right?"

"Are you serious right now?"

He grins like a demon and I roll my eyes, a relieved laugh slipping out when I realize he's just fucking with me. Looking awfully pleased with himself, he traps his tongue between his teeth and drops the hood from his head, walking over to me to shove his face into mine.

"Just so you know, I might not be your boyfriend, but I *am* yours, which means you have to be mine, too." He fists my jacket, pulling me down to his eye level. "And if you fuck anyone else like you almost fucked Arianna last night, I'll never give you my ass again."

I raise a brow and he kisses me, then he bends over to grab his bag and heads for the stairs.

"Maybe I'll just take it," I call after him, smirking when he stops half way up and stares at me over his shoulder, his eyes darkening with something that looks a lot like heat.

Dirty little brat.

CHAPTER 16

NICKY

I LOOK up from my notebook just in time to see Kade checking every aisle on his way through the library, stopping mid step when he sees me sitting here.

"There you are," he hisses, ignoring the several stares he's getting for being too loud, quickly checking me for damage as he walks over to my table. "What the fuck are you doing in here?"

"It's study hall, Kade," I say slowly. "I'm studying."

"Study hall ended twenty minutes ago, Nicky," he grits out, snatching the pen I'm chewing on to toss it into my school bag. "Get up. We're going to lunch."

"But I'm not—"

His eyes hit mine and I snap my mouth shut, sighing loudly as I stand up to pack my shit away. Pulling my sleeves down to my knuckles, I shove my hands into my front pocket and follow him out to the hall, side-eyeing him with a small grin when I realize how mad he is.

"You alright, brother?"

His jaw ticks and he carries on walking, waiting to ensure no one hears before he decides to answer. "I swear to god you do this shit to me on purpose."

"I do not," I lie, laughing lightly when he turns his head to glare at me. "Okay, maybe."

He makes a noise and pushes the cafeteria door open, gesturing to one of the few empty tables in the back corner. "What do you want?"

"A little of everything," I joke, but I don't think he finds me funny. "Whatever's fine."

He goes to wait in line and I shake my head at him, not missing the eyes on my back as I choose a table and drop my ass down. I take my notebook out and finish the paragraph I was writing before I forget it, looking up when I spot Mark, Parker and Austin walking towards me with their trays in their hands.

"Do you ever do anything besides homework and jerk off?" Parker teases, sitting down on the bench seat next to me as Mark and Austin take the one opposite. "In that order, too, am I right?"

I don't have an answer for that, which is why I close my book and rest my forearms on top of it, lamely playing with my sleeves just so I have something to do with my hands. I don't mind these boys and the sly digs they throw my way when Kade's not around—not as much as I used to, at least—but I can't look them in the eye when they crowd my space like this, too afraid they'll accuse me of checking them out if I stare for too long.

Kade finally walks over with two plates of pasta and sets one down in front of me, staring blankly at the side of Parker's face until he takes the hint. Parker rolls his eyes but laughs it off, scooting around to the other side of the table to sit next to Mark. Kade takes his seat beside me and I pick up my fork, smiling to myself while I play with the food on my plate.

"You good?" he asks me, keeping his voice low to ensure the boys don't hear.

I nod and he licks his lips, discreetly looking over his shoulder to check no one's watching, then he takes a sip of his water and rests his left hand on my lap. My skin tingles beneath my jeans and I squeeze my legs together, looking down to find him crooking a finger in his direction. Quick to obey my older brother, I clear my throat and scoot a little closer to him, doing my best not to shiver when he spreads his fingers out and digs his nails into my thigh.

"Good boy," he mouths, and just like that, my dick is hard and my heart is racing with adrenaline.

I fucking love it when he talks to me like that.

He smirks like he knows it and carries on eating, eyes forward as he pretends to listen to whatever Mark is talking about. I copy him and take a bite of my food, shivering for real this time when he moves his hand up a little higher. I look over at him and he circles my outer thigh with his thumb, his touch gentle and soothing as if he's telling me to keep being good for him.

Jesus, is he *rewarding* me?

Testing the waters, I scoop up another forkful of pasta and shove it into my mouth, fighting a groan when his hand moves higher again, his long fingers brushing the inside of my thigh this time. He squeezes me there and I almost choke on my own tongue, but I don't stop eating, afraid he'll pull away if I don't give him what he wants. By the time I've eaten almost all of it, his hand is just below my dick and I'm so close to going off in my jeans, *so* close that I have to stop for a second to take a drink, genuinely afraid he's about to out us in front of the entire school. I risk a glance at him and he slides his hand around to my back, gently tracing the bottom of my spine with his fingertips. He's still not looking at me, but I don't miss what he's trying to tell me without words.

He won't out us.

He knows my body just as well as he knows his own, and there's no way he's about to push me that far, to make me come in front of everyone here.

But *fuck*, I need to come.

Like now.

"Nicky liked her," someone says, and I'm suddenly pulled back to the conversation I haven't been paying attention to, blinking at Austin in confusion.

"I… what?"

"That emo girl I fucked at the cabin," he explains, wiggling his brows at me. "You liked her, right?"

My cheeks heat with embarrassment and I drop my eyes to my plate, not forgetting the look he gave me when I all but ran away from her the other night. Kade tenses beside me and moves his hand back to where it was before, making me jump a little bit, his touch quickly morphing from teasing to possessive.

And *pissed.*

Fuck, he looks pissed.

Unaware of my brother's death glare pointed his way, Austin cocks his head at me, still waiting for an answer to his question, it seems.

"She was okay," I finally say, rolling my eyes when all three boys laugh and shake their heads at me.

Whatever.

The conversation moves on and I finish the last few bites of my lunch, focusing on Kade and his hand in my lap, desperately trying to keep still for him. As soon as I drop my fork on my empty plate, he squeezes the base of my cock and I bite down hard on my bottom lip, a tiny little whimper slipping out before I can stop it.

Fuck.

"Shh," he whispers, so quiet I can barely hear him.

I breathe a little faster and he runs his palm over the length of my dick, slowly slipping his fingers between my legs to tease my hole. My eyes widen and I snatch his wrist, looking up to find him staring at something across the room, a tiny hint of a smirk on his face as he carries on playing with me beneath the table. I frown and follow his line of sight, finding Jasper sitting with a couple seniors a few feet away, hiding a massive grin behind his knuckles as he stares right back at us.

Shit.

<hr>

"Come here, baby," he rasps, shoving me back against the wall in the boy's locker room, easily lifting my legs up around his waist. "You've got three minutes."

"I don't *need* three minutes," I whine, digging my heels into his hips to fuck his fist. "Kade."

"I got you," he assures me, spitting into his free hand to shove it beneath my jeans, rubbing my hole with two wet fingers to set me off.

"Oh, god."

"*There* you go…" he draws out, sliding his tongue over my lips. "Now, be a good boy and give me your neck."

My mouth falls wide open and I tip my head back with a loud moan, my eyebrows pinched together while I come for him within seconds.

"Baby, are you bi?" he asks, sucking my pulse into his mouth, so hard I'm sure he's marking me.

"I… *fuck.*"

"You can tell me," he whispers, teasing the spot with his teeth. "I won't be mad at you."

"I'm not bi," I choke out, clinging on to his shoulders to keep myself steady. "I didn't want her. I just…"

"You just what?"

"She had pretty eyes."

"She had pretty eyes," he echoes, pulling back a bit to look at me. "What the hell does that mean?"

Not wanting to talk about this, I slide my tongue over his and he groans into my mouth, dropping my legs from his waist to push me down to my knees. I pull his jeans down as quickly as I can and he takes his cock out, rubbing his knuckles all over it to use my cum as lube.

"Open."

I do as I'm told and he jerks off right above my face,

raking his fingers through my hair to keep me still. I lick around my lips and he curses, squeezing his dick to slide the length over my tongue.

"Swallow it," he orders, and then he's coming, coating the inside of my mouth with our combined release.

I wrap my lips around him and suck on the tip, greedy for everything he's willing to give me, wanting every single drop. I take his dick in my hand and lick it from the base to the tip, but then he yanks my head back by my hair and glares at something on my throat.

"Shit," he hisses, quickly pulling me back up to my feet, snatching a couple paper towels from the dispenser to clean us both up. "Fucking *shit*."

"What's wrong?" I ask, struggling not to panic when I catch the look in his eyes.

It's fear, and it scares the shit out of me.

He takes my face in his hands and runs his thumb over the side of my neck, leaning over me like he's trying to shield me from the outside world and everyone in it. "Keep this covered and stay away from Jasper," he says quietly, leaving absolutely no room for argument. "Stay away from *everyone*, you hear me?"

I nod rapidly and swallow the lump in my throat, fisting my collar to hide the hickey he just gave me. "Okay."

CHAPTER 17

KADE

IT'S STORMING OUTSIDE TONIGHT, so bad they've had to close the main road leading out of town thanks to a fallen tree that almost hit a moving car. The fights were called off considering we can't get to the woods without being seen by the cops manning the roadblock, our dad being one of them, but I don't mind.

I like storms.

They remind me of Mom and Nicky and blankets and hot chocolate, freezing cold nights on the couch in front of the shitty fireplace, the three of us curled up together while we ate popcorn and watched movies.

I take my headphones out so I can hear the rain beating against the window, leaning back on my bed to finish typing up this essay I have due on Monday. I manage to get a few more sentences written, but I can't help the way my eyes keep drifting to the bathroom door on my left, my heart sinking a little further every time I think about what I did to him at school the other day.

I need to be more careful with him.

Fuck that.

I need to stop *touching* him, right now before he gets caught with my goddamn mark on his neck.

I don't think anyone saw it, but still, that was fucking stupid.

Unable to concentrate with this awful mix of *feelings* rushing through me, I abandon my essay and stand up to walk to the bathroom. I know I shouldn't, because I need to *stop*, but my body's moving by itself and I don't have it in me to fight it any longer.

I'm so sick of fighting.

I push the door open and squint at the thick cloud of steam filling the room, frowning when Nicky curses and drops the little black pencil he's holding. His hair's still wet and the water's still running, but he's not *in* the shower like I thought he was—like he tried to *fool* me into thinking he was.

Fully clothed in a pair of sweats and a hoodie, he bends down to grab what he dropped and stashes it beneath the screwed up towel next to the sink, tucking his chin down to his chest to hide his face from me.

"What are you doing?"

"I didn't... y-you're supposed to be writing," he stammers, blindly reaching over to grab a couple tissues from the side. "Did you finish alread—

"Look at me."

He shakes his head no and I reach over to turn the shower off, slowly walking over to him to press my hips to his. I trap him between me and the counter and take his jaw with one hand, raising a brow when he tightens it, locking it up to ensure his head stays down. I'm stronger than he is, though, and it barely takes any effort at all to overpower him. I push his head back with a little more force than necessary and study his pale face, my mood quickly shifting from wary to infuriated when I spot the black shit covering his eyes. My own eyes darken and I dig my fingers into his jaw, my nostrils flaring at the sight of my little brother wearing fucking *makeup*.

"What is that?"

"It's—" he cuts off, his cheeks *burning* with embarrassment and shame. "It's eyeliner."

"I know *what* it is, Nicky," I grit out, unable to control my temper. "Why the fuck is it on your face?"

He doesn't answer that, and it's only now I realize how hard he's shaking, holding his breath as he white knuckles the edge of the counter either side of him.

She had pretty eyes.

"I'm sorry," he blurts out, but I'm already losing it, ripping my fingers through his hair to pull his mouth up to mine.

"*Mine.*"

He whimpers and I feed him my tongue, sliding my other hand beneath his waistband, squeezing his ass to rub him against me. Feeling his cock thicken through the thick layers of our clothes, I shove his leg out with my knee and drag his thigh up to my hip, grinding on him and dry fucking him into the counter.

"*Mine,*" I tell him again, making him moan.

"Kade," he says, and even though I know he's confused as to what the fuck I'm doing, hearing my name on his lips only makes me crazier.

I pull his teeth down with my thumb and lick the inside of his mouth, needing to *own* him, enjoying the way he submits for me without having to be told.

"Good boy," I whisper, shamelessly feeding that little praise kink of his, knowing it'll make him do whatever I tell him to do. "You gonna choke on my dick?"

He drops to his knees and I smirk, pushing his hair back from his forehead so I can see his eyes while I use his throat. He swallows me whole and I groan, leaning one hand against the edge of the counter while I hold the top of his head with the other.

I was supposed to *stop*, goddamnit.

I know nothing good can come of this.

We're *brothers*, for fuck's sake.

It doesn't matter that we don't share the same blood when we've shared the same *everything* since we were three years old. The same house, the same parents, the same last name, the same fucking *bath tub*…

If anyone ever finds out about us, they'll call us incest.

Disgusting.

Dirty fucking faggots.

The thought only makes me fuck him harder.

He gags on my cock and I grit my teeth, forcing myself not to come when I catch the black streaks dripping from his eyes. I pull him off of me and he gasps, lifting his sleeves to wipe the spit from his chin.

"Does that feel good?"

I open my mouth to tell him it feels better than fucking *good*, snapping it shut again when I realize he's not just asking for the sake of it—he really wants to know.

Without warning, I fist his collar and pull him up to his feet, stealing another kiss from his wet mouth as I take him back to my room. I lie him down on the bed and kneel on the mattress between his legs, bunching his hoodie up to his collarbone to run my mouth over his nipples. I slide my tongue down over his flesh and circle his navel, then I move across to his hip bone to nip it with my teeth. Just as I knew he would, he bucks his ass up and I take full advantage, pulling his sweats and boxers down to his ankles in one quick move. I toss them away and take his cock in my hand, looking up at him while I lick his head, tasting the precum there. His eyes widen when he realizes what I'm doing and he curses, lifting himself up on his elbows to fist the sheet with both hands.

"Kade..." he warns, and I grin like a maniac, opening my mouth as wide as I can to wrap my lips around him.

He shouts something that doesn't make sense and I suck without remorse, moving up and down, again and again, a little more each time until I've got him balls deep inside me. He's not as big as I am, but having a dick wedged at the back of my throat still makes me gag, my head spinning at the lack of oxygen in my lungs. Mimicking what he does to me, I breathe through my nose and force myself to relax, laughing lightly when he thrashes around like he's being tortured.

"Keep still," I mumble around his cock, taking the backs of his knees to pin them to the bed either side of him.

Right then, his eyes roll back in his head and he shivers violently, his hands taking hold of my hair and *pulling*, hard enough to burn my motherfucking scalp.

"*Kade.*"

"What, Nicky?" I ask, not really expecting an answer considering he's lost his damn mind, but then it hits me and I laugh some more. "You like it when I talk?"

He moans loudly and I take that as a yes, allowing him to make as much noise as he wants because the storm's louder, anyway. The neighbors won't hear him over that, and if they do… well, I'll deal with them later.

"Put your feet flat on the bed and fuck my mouth," I demand. "All the fucking way, baby."

He makes that needy little sound I love and tightens his grip on my hair, looking a little dizzy, then he does what I told him to and rolls his hips out, fucking himself into my waiting throat. I gag again and hold myself up on my forearms, opening my mouth as wide as it'll go, giving him free reign to take whatever he wants from me.

"God," he rasps, leaning up to watch what he's doing, pausing for a second to allow me to breathe.

His eyes hit mine and *fuck me*, I'll suck his dick every day for the rest of my life if it makes him look at me like that, like *I'm* his god, the only fucking thing he can see.

"Does that feel good?" I taunt, pulling off of him to suck the tip into my mouth.

"Oh, shit—I mean, *fuck*. Yes. Yeah, it feels… *fuck*."

Knowing he's about to come, I pull back all the way and tap his outer thigh. "Turn over."

"What?"

Instead of repeating myself, I snatch his hips and flip him onto his stomach, roughly smacking his ass before I lift him up to his knees. He lets out a squeal and I spread his cheeks with my thumbs, fucking loving how soft his flesh feels beneath my fingertips. His breathing picks up and he looks at me over his shoulder, but he doesn't get to ask what I'm doing before I dip my head and flick his hole with my tongue.

"Oh, fuck," he chokes out, face planting the bed to bite the covers, curling his body to arch himself into my face.

I do it again and he starts to shake, moaning and begging around the fabric between his teeth. I groan and squeeze the backs of his thighs, pushing them outwards to get the angle I want.

"Give me your hands."

He does and I take his wrists, folding his arms behind his back to pin them to his spine. I spit on his ass and spread his hole with my thumb and forefinger, pushing my tongue inside to fuck him with it. That drives him wild and he bucks against me, but there's nowhere for him to go when I have him trapped like this—mine to do whatever I damn well please with.

Fucking mine.

Still shaking and moaning, he digs his nails into his forearms and I reach down between his legs, wrapping my hand around his cock to jerk him off. I work him over just like that until I feel his body lock up with tension—right fucking *there*—then I straighten up and pull his back to my chest, digging my fingers into his hair to suck and bite on his lips.

"Fuck, you fucking prick," he growls, grinding himself against me, desperately moving his ass up and down on my lap. "Damn it, Kade, why are you edging me?"

"Punishment."

"Punishment for what?" he complains, whimpering into my mouth. "You said I was good."

"I know I did, baby," I say softly, turning his head until he's facing me fully, running my thumb over the black beneath his eye. "Doesn't mean I have to like it."

He whines and I kiss him, tangling my tongue with his while I lower him down to his back. He tugs at my shirt and I pull it off over my head, tossing it down next to his jeans before I do the same with the rest of our clothes. Lying down between his legs, I run my hand over his side and lick his lips, reaching over to grab the lube I stashed in my nightstand. I pour some onto my fingers and stretch him out slowly, watching his face for his reaction while I get him ready for my cock.

"I didn't use a condom that night."

"And?"

I raise a brow at that, twisting my hand to add a second finger. "You trust me that much?"

"I trust you with my life, Kade," he says simply, his mouth parting at the feel of my fingers crooking inside him. "I wouldn't have been that stupid if it were anyone else, but—" he cuts off, wincing when I wrap my hand around his neck and squeeze. "Fuck. I'm sorry."

"You will be," I taunt, pulling my fingers out to line my dick up with his hole. "Who else are you gonna let fuck you, Nicky?"

"No one," he rasps. "No one but you."

"Why not?"

"Because I'm yours."

"For how long?"

"Always."

I groan and slip my way inside him, releasing my grip on his throat to wrap my hand around his cock. He cries out and digs his fingers into my shoulders, his dark eyebrows dipped in concentration as he focuses on breathing, slowly pulling me all the way in.

"That's it," I praise, leaning over him to lick the corner of his mouth. "Such a good little slut for me."

He whimpers a curse and I ease him into it, fucking him long and slow before I work it up to hard and deep. My headboard bangs against the wall with every hit but I don't stop, telling myself I'll just have to kill any neighbor who looks at him twice tomorrow.

And I will.

For Nicky, I'd do anything.

But that's not true, is it?

I'd kill for him in a second, but I wouldn't die or go to jail for him. Not because I don't love him enough, but because there *is* no world where he exists without me in it.

He needs me and I need him.

Fucking always.

"Kade," he pleads, bringing me back to the present,

roughly dragging his nails over my back. "Shit, Kade, I'm gonna come. Please, don't fucking stop."

I couldn't if I wanted to.

Finally putting him out of his misery, I sit back on my heels and lift him up with me, spreading his legs out over my lap without pulling out. "Don't let go, okay?"

He nods and locks his arms around my head, his greedy little mouth attacking mine like he's starving for me. I kiss him back and squeeze his ass with my free hand, jerking him off while I fuck up into him, searching for that spot that'll make him scream for me. Just as I think it, he comes loudly and I'm right there with him, my vision clouding at the feel of his ass pulsing around my cock, stealing the cum from my dick.

"Fuck, baby," I growl, bucking against him when I feel him tearing at my neck. "Vicious little bastard."

He lets out a sound crossed between a laugh and a sob, losing his grip on me as his body goes limp in my arms. I catch him by his waist and ease him down to the pillows, lying on my side beside him to pull the blanket up to our shoulders. His eyes fall closed and I guide his thigh over my hip, running the tips of my fingers over his face, studying the makeup there.

"Why do you have to be so fucking beautiful?" I whisper, moving my thumb down to trace his lips.

"You want me to be ugly?"

"It'd make my life easier," I mutter, making him laugh for real this time, his mouth splitting into a big ass grin as he cracks an eye open to look at me.

"You're a jealous fucker."

I make a noise and drop my face to his neck, inhaling his scent while I play with the soft strands of his hair.

"Kade?" he asks after a while, his voice barely audible.

"Yeah?"

"Do you think Mom would hate us?"

"Mom's not here," I say vaguely, sliding my tongue over his hickey to distract him, ignoring the kick in my gut that makes me feel like a sick piece of shit.

"Kade."

I sigh and pull back to look him in the eye, not even bothering to insult him with lies. "Yes, baby, she'd hate us," I admit, ghosting my lips over his to soften the sting. "We're her sons. *Fucking*. Fucking *gay*. Just because she wasn't a bitch to us doesn't mean she would have been okay with this. It's wrong, Nicky."

He nods because he knew all that already, trapping his lip between his teeth as if he's trying to stop it from shaking. "I miss her, Kade."

"I know you do," I croak out, swallowing the emotion creeping up my throat while I wrap my arms around his body. "I miss her, too, baby boy."

CHAPTER 18

KADE

Thirteen years old…

"Kade, honey, will you help me with this, please?" Mom asks, helplessly holding her left hand to her chest as she looks down at the full trash can in front of her.

I grit my teeth and stand up to go to her, leaving Nicky to do his math homework at the kitchen table.

I'm not mad at her for asking. I'm mad at her for lying to my face when I asked what happened to her mangled finger when we got home from school today.

She told me she tripped.

She's always fucking tripping.

Refusing to look directly at me, she sits down beside Nicky and places her good hand on his shoulder, jumping like a mouse caught in a trap when Dad's voice comes from the doorway behind her.

"What do you think you're doing?" he asks, staring at her pale face, then moving his eyes to mine.

"Taking the trash out," I answer, silently praying he just nods and carries on walking.

Of course he doesn't do that, though.

"You're making our son do your job *for* you?" he draws out, raising a dark, amused brow at her. "While you what, help the nerdy one with his fucking fractions?"

"I wasn't helping h—"

"Do not interrupt me, Sara!" he shouts, stepping closer to wave a hand in my direction. "I work my ass off to pay the bills around here and you do *nothing*, you lazy bitch. Get off your bony ass and do it yourself."

"Her finger's broken, Dad," I spit out, bravely lifting my chin as I step between the two of them, looking up at his angry face and feeling nothing but anger myself. "Because, you know, she *tripped*."

He glares and swings for my face, but then I hear a shriek followed by the sound of wood scraping on wood, my shoulder hitting the freezer just as his fist catches my mother on the mouth.

"Mom!"

She falls down on her side and I crouch down beside her, swinging my head around to Nicky when he shoots up from his seat like he's about to rush over to us.

"Get upstairs."

"But—"

"*Now*, Nicky."

He flinches and stares at me with glassy eyes, hesitating for five seconds too long before he snatches his notebook and makes a beeline for the hallway. Dad laughs to himself and mutters something I don't catch, too busy worrying about my mom and brother to pay attention to whatever he's saying. He steps closer again and Mom uses the chair to pull herself up, lifting her hands in defeat as she blocks his path to me.

"I'll do it," she rasps, paying no mind to the blood dripping over her chin. "I'll do it, okay?"

He cocks his head and crosses his arms over his chest, watching her closely while she ties the trash bag with shaky fingers, cursing herself when she doesn't get it right the first time, or the second. My nostrils flare and I grind my teeth, unable to do shit but stand here and watch her struggle. It takes her a minute, but she finally gets it done and carries the bag outside, rushing now to ensure I'm not left alone with him for too long. As soon as she comes back, he squeezes her left hand and kisses the wound on her mouth, making her wince.

"I'll see you tomorrow, my love."

"Okay, darling," she manages, smiling through the pain like she always does. "Be careful out there."

He smirks and backs away from her, licking the blood from his lip while he grabs his keys and leaves for the night shift. The front door closes behind him and she lets out a sob, quickly snapping a hand over her mouth to hide it from me. I already heard it, but I don't say anything while I run my hand over her back, doing my best to make her feel safe and loved as I guide her toward the stairs. We walk to the top and find Nicky standing there with his back to the wall, his shoulders dropping with relief when he sees us. Knowing what to do by now, he helps me guide her to her bedroom and sets her down on the edge of the bed, stumbling over the corner of the rug as he walks to our parents' bathroom.

"Damn it."

I shake my head at him and push the hair back from my mother's face, carefully sitting down next to her to take her good hand in mine. "Why do you stay with him, Mom?" I ask quietly, looking down to stare at the older bruises on her arms and wrists.

I don't want her to leave us, but I have to know.

"My sweet boy," she says softly, taking my cheek to pull my eyes back to hers. "Do you think he'd let me take you with me?"

I shake my head and she smiles sadly, her silent tears falling over her cheeks and neck. "That's why."

I swallow and clear the lump in my throat, looking over when Nicky falls over the rug again, almost dropping the glass of water he's holding.

"Fucking thing," he hisses, huffing to himself as he walks back over to us, blushing a little bit when Mom raises a brow at him. "Sorry."

She manages a light laugh and accepts the pills he gives her, tossing them into her mouth before taking the water from his hand. "Thank you, sweetheart."

He nods and we take care of her the best we can, wiping the blood away with a warm washcloth, then cleaning her up with the hydrogen peroxide Nicky grabbed from the bathroom. By the time the three of us are curled up in bed together, Nicky's eyelids give up on him and he falls asleep on my lap, lying on his front between my legs with his arms wrapped around my waist.

"Does he always lie on you like that?" Mom whispers, rolling her head to the side to look at me. "When you're alone, I mean. Does he touch you like that a lot?"

I frown and run my hands through his hair, stopping when I realize she's staring at his mouth next to my thigh, her lip curling like she's tasted something dirty.

I don't want to lie to her, but something tells me the truth isn't an option for me right now.

"No, he's just upset."

She nods slowly and seems to rid whatever she was thinking about, quiet a minute before she speaks again. "Your brother's a troubled boy, Kade," she tells me, her voice so small I can barely hear it over the ringing in my ears. "Have you noticed that?

"No."

But I have, and I think she knows it.

"He listens to you," she goes on, struggling to keep her eyes open thanks to whatever was in those pills she loves so much. "When the time comes, I need you to pull him back for me, okay? I need you to fix him before it's too late."

Before she has no choice, she means.

Before she and everyone else turn their backs on him and leave him to the wolves.

My jaw ticks and I stare at the side of his beautiful face, thankful she doesn't wait for me to say anything back before she passes out on my shoulder.

I don't think he heard what she said about him, but I still hold him extra tight for a while, silently promising him that no matter what happens, *I'll* never leave him, that I'll set the goddamn world on fire before I let anything bad happen to him.

And I fucking mean it, too.

CHAPTER 19

NICKY

"WHAT ARE YOU THINKING ABOUT, BROTHER?" I ask, not missing the eyes following my every move as I shove my arms through my sleeves.

He's sitting down at the kitchen table with his elbows resting on the cheap wood, his dark hair falling over his forehead as he moves his gaze over my form.

"Is it me?" I joke, lifting the hem of my hoodie to show him my abs. "It's me, isn't it?"

He raises a brow but keeps his thoughts to himself, running his tongue over his bottom lip while he stares at the front of my jeans. Tired of being ignored, I let go of my hoodie and step closer to him.

"Lean back."

Seemingly amused by me and my demand, he does as he's told and takes my hand, pulling me in to stand between his open thighs. I lift my leg up and straddle his lap, placing my hands on both sides of his face to steal a heated kiss from his mouth.

He doesn't usually say much as it is, but he's been extra moody this past week, zoning out all the time as if there's something slowly eating away at him.

I don't like it, and I'm constantly terrified he's about to pull the rug out from under me and break my heart.

Because that's exactly what'll happen if he decides to end this thing between us.

I don't want it to end.

Luckily for me, though, *not* being with me seems to be the last thing on his mind right now.

He squeezes my ass and I moan into his mouth, sliding my hands through his hair to pull on it. He uses his palms to guide me and I follow his lead, rolling my hips out to rub our dicks together, jumping right back off of him when I hear a key turning in the front door.

Fuck.

He quickly tosses me a dish cloth and scoots himself back under the table, taking his phone out to pull up some random model's Instagram feed. I scrunch my nose and turn away from him, doing my best to ignore my stupid jealousy while I wipe the surfaces we just cleaned a half hour ago.

"Oh, hi, boys," Elle says, her sickly sweet smile fading when we say nothing back. "What are you up to?"

Again, nothing.

I keep my eyes on my task and do my best to calm my erratic heartbeat, thankful my hoodie covers my zipper and hides how hard I am beneath my jeans.

"Okay, well, I, uh, saw your new friend at the store

just now," she informs us, dropping her grocery bag on the counter to pull her things out. "Jasper, is it?"

"He's not our friend," Kade mutters, his tone flat while he continues scrolling on his phone.

"Really?" she asks, turning to look at him over her shoulder. "Because he seems to know the two of you *very* well."

Kade's jaw ticks and he lifts his eyes up, slowly standing from his chair to walk over to her. "Do you have something to say to us, little girl?" he asks cruelly, towering over her small frame. "Because if you do, stop playing and spit it the fuck out."

She swallows and looks at me, clearly not brave or stupid enough to meet his stare head on. "Nicky, can I talk to you alone for a minute, please?"

"No, you can't," Kade answers for me, backing away from her to grab his keys from the side.

He tilts his head at me and I toss the cloth into the sink, throwing my hood over my head while I follow him to the front door. She doesn't say anything else or try to stop us from leaving, but I can feel her judgy little eyes on our backs as we make our way outside.

"What the fuck was that?" I whisper to him, dipping my head to protect my face from the rain.

"She thinks I'm hurting you."

"Yes, I'm aware of that, Kade," I say dryly, hopping up to the passenger side of the truck. "I meant *why*? Do you think Jasper said something to her?"

"I don't know."

"You don't know," I echo, shaking my head at his bullshit attitude, nervously looking around to check she's not still watching us. "I don't like this, man. What if—"

"Nicky, stop," he cuts in, taking my hand while he drives towards the lights at the end of the street. "No one's seen us together, okay? They can think what they want but they can't prove shit. We just need to be more careful."

I nod and fumble with the dial to turn the heat on, my teeth chattering at the cold chill that never seems to leave my body.

Careful.

Right.

We can do that.

"KADE, YOU'RE UP," SKULLY CALLS, CROOKING A FINGER AT him while he nudges the other guy towards the pit.

This one's a huge, older looking dude with a man bun and a dark beard cut down to his chest, his thick body covered in black leather and scars and tattoos. I can't see from here, but I'm almost sure he had snake eye contacts in when he looked at me a minute ago.

"Kade?"

"What, Nicky?"

"How old is that guy?"

"Who cares?" he throws back, pulling his shirt over his head to pass it to me, placing a hand on my shoulder to set me down on the log. "Keep your ass right there."

"Yes, Dadd—"

His eyes hit mine and I roll my lips with my fingertips, hiding a grin while I watch him back away from me. He shakes his head and then turns around, ignoring the huge crowd on the sidelines while he walks towards the guy he's fighting. As soon as it starts, the rest of the world seems to blur and all I see is my older brother, my eyes zoned in on the way his abs and arms flex with every swing he takes, the way he laughs every time the other guy takes a swing right back at him. The giant fucker manages to get a few hits in here and there, most of them to his face, but Kade doesn't seem to mind. He just spits on the ground and carries on going, smirking at him as if he's baiting him to do it again.

He's so fucking hot.

Just then, something catches my eye and I blink, looking over to find Jasper standing behind me. He wiggles his brows and opens his mouth to say something, but then a scream fills my ears followed by several gasps and shouts, the majority of the crowd taking a few steps back as one. I panic and whip my head around to Kade, jumping up to my feet when I spot the fucking knife in the other guy's hand. Kade lifts his hands up to his shoulders and dips his head to study the fresh cut on his abs, the small drop of blood travelling down to his waistband, then he raises that dark eyebrow and looks up at the stupid prick in front of him.

Oh, fuck.

Before he can even think about his next move, Kade grabs the guy's arm with his left hand and snatches the knife from his grip, smashing his elbow into his nose at the same time, probably breaking it. The guy shouts out a curse and drops to his knees, cupping his bleeding face while Kade walks over to me. He tosses me the knife and I fumble to catch it, quickly pulling him back by his wrist when he turns around again.

"What?" he asks, looking at me over his shoulder.

"Don't kill him."

"I won't."

"Or *almost* kill him."

He smirks at that, his eyes lighting up with something that looks a lot like excitement. Knowing there's no point trying to talk sense into him, I let him go with a flick of my wrist and drop my ass back down, shoving the knife into my pocket before I lean over to grab my drink. The fight goes on and I watch Kade lay into him again and again, thankful Jasper decided to get the fuck out of sight before Kade saw him.

"You little cunt!" the guy on the floor growls, and I snort out a laugh, cringing when Kade leans over to grab his arm with both hands, one on his wrist and the other by his elbow. "No! Fucking hell, *stop*! I'm sorry! I'm—"

The crunch of bone breaking fills my ears and I look away, struggling not to gag on the beer in my mouth.

Fucking gross.

I dip my head to spit it out on the floor, and then the grown ass man screams—literally *screams* loud enough to wake the dead. He bangs his good fist against the ground and Skully finally calls it, laughing beside me when the crowd loses their motherfucking minds. I swipe the cash from his hand and take a step back, attempting to get away from the full on riot breaking out in front of me. I look around and almost fall over my own feet, grinning when Kade appears out of nowhere and wraps his arms around my waist, feeling me all over as if he's checking for injury.

"You okay?"

"No, that was disgusting," I shout. *"You're disgusting."*

He laughs at me and takes my forearm, grabbing his things from the ground before he pulls me along with him, the two of us ducking our heads to avoid the branches and rocks being thrown about. We make a run for it and he takes me around to the front of the old church, only slowing his pace once we're hidden from the group of raging lunatics behind us. Knowing he's about to head straight for the truck, I dig my heels into the dirt and drag him up to the rotting iron doors at the top of the steps, ignoring his frown while I shove my way inside.

"What are you doing?"

"Dad and Elle are home tonight," I explain, sliding my hands around his neck to pull his mouth down to mine.

"Nicky," he groans, shaking his head no, but his freezing cold fingers have no problem finding their way beneath my hoodie, his nails digging themselves into my back. "Fuck, baby, this isn't careful."

"No one's here."

"Someone could catch us."

"No one's here," I repeat, gently sucking his lip between my teeth, taunting him. "Don't you want me?"

Instead of answering with words, he picks me up by my waist and carries me to the corner of the church, setting me down in front of the pews that have been ripped from the floor and tossed aside. "What do *you* want, baby brother?"

I smirk and start to tell him I want his cock in my ass, but then I hesitate, looking up at him through my lashes. "Promise you won't get mad if I tell you?"

He nods, and I pray to god he means it.

"I want more," I admit, my heart pumping against my ribcage while I ready myself to throw it all out there, to well and truly ruin my relationship with the only brother I'll ever have. "More nights—no, *every* night. I want you to love me the way I've loved you since before I knew what it meant. I want—"

He kisses me before I can finish and steals all the air from my lungs, dropping his things to the floor before he walks me back another step. "What else?" he rasps, his lips never leaving mine. "Tell me the last part."

"I want you to take me away and never let me go."

As soon as I've said it, he spins me around and pulls my back to his chest, his hands roaming my sides while he drops his face to my neck. "You know I can't give you that, Nicky," he whispers, kissing me there. "We can't just *be* together. Not like that. Not *forever.*"

"No, but we'll do it, anyway," I say simply, lifting my arms up to wrap them around his head. "Right, brother?"

His lips stretch into a grin against my flesh and I take that as a yes, shivering against him when he moves his mouth to my ear. "You really went all out on me, huh?"

I smile shyly at that, twisting my head around to look at him. "Yeah, well, I still want you to fuck me."

"We don't have lube."

"I don't care."

"You sure?" he teases, rubbing his fingers over my hole through my sweats. "It's gonna burn like fuck without it."

"I said I don't care," I grit out, whimpering when he presses down a little harder. "I'm sorry."

"You gonna keep giving me attitude?"

"No."

He pushes me forward until my hips hit the pew nearest the wall, shoving my waistband down to my thighs before he lifts his palm up to my mouth. I spit on it and he moves behind me, holding me still by the back of my neck as he slides his fingers over my ass. Just as he slides the tips in, he bends me over and spits on it himself, rimming me with his tongue to get me as wet as possible.

"God," I choke out, squeezing my eyes shut while I stand up on my tiptoes, spreading my legs out with my hands flat on the seat in front of me.

"*God*?" he echoes, his tone laced with humor. "Really?"

I breathe a laugh and look up at the walls, only just realizing the rain is falling through the several cracks in the roof. It's not enough to soak us completely, but enough that I'll probably wake up with a cold tomorrow. *Church* by Fall Out Boy plays somewhere in the distance and I focus on that, opening my mouth while Kade stretches me out with his fingers. Straightening up to his full height, he curls them downward and I moan through my teeth, shifting my legs out some more to grab my aching dick. He smacks my wrist and I jump, shaking my head at him when I realize why he did it.

"That's mine," he tells me, roughly pulling me back to his chest, lifting his hand back to my mouth. "More."

I spit on it again and he rubs it all over his cock, pressing his thighs to the backs of mine while he teases my hole with the head. I writhe impatiently and he squeezes my waist, forcing yet another moan from my throat. I keep still this time and he pushes it in, forcing his way inside until his hips bump my ass. I wince before I can stop it and bite down on my lip, digging my nails into the pew until my knuckles turn white.

Fuck.

Fuck, fuck, fuck.

"You asked for this, you know?" he taunts me, pulling out a little bit just to push it back in, harder this time.

All the breath leaves my lungs and I let my head fall back on his chest, laughing lightly despite the pain I'm in. "Try all you like, brother. You don't scare me."

"No?"

"No," I say honestly. "You never have."

He hums and cups my jaw with his fingers, bringing my face around to touch my lips with his. "Last chance to tell me to pull out, baby boy. Because as soon as I start fucking this slutty little hole, I'm not fucking stopping."

Jesus.

"I thought you said you'd just take it," I remind him, purposely riling him up. "Was that just bullshi—"

Faster than I can blink, he takes my dick out fully and moves his other hand to my throat, holding me tight against him while he takes me hard and fucking deep. I cry out into his mouth and hold on to his wrist, my eyes rolling at the way he's stretching me raw. He was right—it burns like a motherfucker—but I still find myself pushing my ass back into his pelvis, silently begging him for more. Without slowing his pace, he slides his tongue from my lips to my neck, swirling it around just beneath my earlobe. My vision blurs and I roll my head from side to side, feeling high and dizzy at the feel of him touching me everywhere, *owning* me everywhere as if it's just second nature to him. My cock throbs in his hand and he groans in my ear, squeezing it once before he swipes his thumb over the precum there.

"Fuck, Nicky," he breathes out, sounding just as unhinged as I am. "You like it when I hurt you?"

"Yes," I moan, desperately rubbing my back against his chest. "Oh my god, Kade, fuck me harder."

He curses and gives me what I need, switching hands to choke me with four fingers, forcing me to taste myself as he smashes my thighs into the wood. I don't have to look down to know he's leaving marks on me, bruising my flesh with this fucking pew while the party goes on less than fifty feet away.

"Kade."

"I got you," he whispers, jerking me off hit for hit, his arms around me the only thing keeping me from falling over. "Let go for me, baby. Fucking scream for me."

I come with a strangled out cry and he pushes down on my tongue, making me gag, my hips spasming while I cover his hand with my cum. Even after I'm finished, he keeps jerking me off and presses his cheek to the side of my face, clearly enjoying the way I'm *vibrating* like a crazy person, instinctively twisting my body in an attempt to get away from him. It's impossible, though, and all I can do is take it like a whore while he takes what he wants from me.

"Such a good little boy," he praises, scraping his teeth across my jaw. "Do you have any idea how fucking good you make me feel? How fucking hot you look with your ass full of your big brother's cock?"

I choke a little bit and he pulls my head back by my hair, licking the inside of my mouth while he massages my scalp with his fingertips. He comes inside me and then slowly grinds his hips, fucking it in even deeper, *finally* releasing his grip on my dick to push his cum back in with his fingers.

"I want you to feel me in here all the way home," he says quietly, resting his chin on my shoulder while he pulls my sweats and boxers back into place.

Unable to use my own legs, I fall back on him and close my eyes, holding on to his forearms while he holds me up from behind. He moves quietly and then I'm in the air, wrapping my arms and legs around him to drop my face to his neck. I don't know how long I fall asleep for, but by the time I crack my eyes open, we're almost back at the truck, hidden behind the thick trees just off the main road. I smile to myself and brush his pulse with my nose, knowing he must have carried me the long way around to avoid throwing me over the fence.

"Nicky?"

"Yeah?" I ask, yawning against him.

"Where's the knife?"

"What knife?"

"The one I gave you at the fight."

I pull my brows in and search my front pocket, my movements a little slower than usual thanks to the lack of brain cells I have left. "Damn it."

"What?"

"I lost it."

He chuckles at the pout on my face and carries on walking towards the truck, pulling the driver's side door open to take me up with him.

"Will you buy me a new one?"

"No."

"A gun, then?"

"Not a chance in hell."

I pout some more and curl myself up into a little ball, resting my head on his shoulder while I use his huge coat as a blanket. "You're mean."

"Yeah, and you're accident prone," he mutters, locking our fingers together while he uses his free hand to drive.

I sigh dramatically and close my eyes again. "Am not."

"Kade, stop it," I hiss, slapping a hand over my mouth to stop myself from moaning. "Oh, shit."

"Baby, shut up."

"I'm *trying*, you fucking asshole."

His body shakes with silent laughter and he glances

up from between my legs, giving me this *look* that doesn't suit him while he licks my inner thigh. I jolt and smack his head away, but the horny bastard just pins my forearms to the sheet and comes right back for more.

Dad and Elle are asleep in the room just across the hall, but that doesn't stop him from making out with my body like he'll die if he doesn't, almost as if he's trying to lick every inch of me he can find.

"Kade, I can't take this."

"Bite down on my shirt," he says quietly, tipping his chin at the pillow beside my head.

Hands still trapped either side of me, I twist my neck and take it between my teeth, clenching my jaw as tight as I can while he continues his cruel torture. He's got me naked on my back in the middle of his bed, spread out like a human feast while he gives me hickeys all over. They're on my chest, my ass right next to my hole, the soles of my fucking *feet*—really small ones that'll pass as bruises if anyone sees. They won't see, because I never take my clothes off in front of anyone but Kade, but still, we're being *careful*.

He gently eats my thigh and I breathe deeply through my nose, curling my fingers into the blanket when he moves his tongue across to the middle of my dick.

"Don't you dare," I grit out, the words muffled by the fabric in my mouth.

"You think it'll work?"

"You're not about to find out."

He smirks and *sucks* on it, making me shake, my sore muscles locking up with every graze of his teeth. After what feels like hours but is probably only a minute or two, he lets go of my arms and takes the base in his hand, grinning at the pink mark he's left there.

"*My* pretty little cock," he says, and I pull the shirt from my mouth, snatching his face to pull him up to me.

I kiss him and he kisses me back, dragging my thigh up to the towel wrapped around his hips, blanketing me with his weight while he moves his lips against mine. He teases the seam with his tongue and I let him in, fucking loving the way he's acting tonight, this playful side of him I don't get to see very often.

I wish it could be like this all the time.

He moves down to my neck and I look up at the ceiling, raking my hand through his damp hair while he worships me with his mouth. He doesn't mark me there, because people *will* see that, and even though I could lie and say some random girl gave it to me, we both know it's not worth the risk of them finding out where it really came from.

"What are you thinking about, baby brother?" he asks, repeating the question I asked him in the kitchen a few hours ago.

"California."

"California," he echoes, pulling back a bit to raise a brow at me. "Is that where you want me to take you?"

"Maybe," I admit, anxiously chewing my lip while I tell him what I found out online the other day. "Did you know Los Angeles is the second gayest city in the country after New York? Two boys can walk the streets holding hands and no one fucking cares, Kade."

"Nicky."

"I know some people *do* care but it's not like it is here," I go on. "And it's far, and warm, and I could get tattoos so no one sees my scars on the beach, and—"

"Nicky," he says again, taking my face to swipe his thumbs over my cheeks. "Baby, why are you crying?"

"I…" I frown, only just feeling the tears leaking from my eyes. "I don't know. I just want us to be safe."

He bites his lip and nods, his own eyes glassing up while he drops his forehead to mine. "We will be."

"So, we can go?" I ask. "Right after graduation?"

"Fuck graduation." He shakes his head, gently bumping my nose with his. "I'll take you as soon as we finish that last exam if that's what you want."

"Do you promise?"

"Have I ever lied to you?"

I shake my head and wipe my eyes with my hands, struggling not to cry even more at the hope rushing through me. I feel like I'm always crying over something, and I probably look like a pathetic loser, but he doesn't call me out on it. Instead he lifts my forearm and moves his tongue over my scarred flesh, digging his teeth into the spot just below my elbow. I moan really quietly and flick his towel open, spreading my legs out to rub my cock against his.

"I love you, Kade," I whisper, but it sounds different this time, a promise and a plea all at once.

"I love you, too, Nicky," he whispers back, and I can't hide my stupid grin, feeding him my arm while I run my fingers over the back of his neck.

He said it different, too.

CHAPTER 20

NICKY

Something feels off today.

I don't feel right, and I can't help but notice the way people are staring at me, whispering shit to each other while they walk around me in the library—*all* the way around me as if I have a disease or some shit.

At first I thought maybe I was imagining it, but it's been happening all morning and it's just getting worse.

"…will you shut up?" a girl from my math class hisses, talking to her friend in one of the aisles. "That's disgusting."

"I'm just telling you what I heard," the other one says, rolling her eyes while she shoves her books up on the top shelf. "Everyone's talking about it."

"Yeah, well, that doesn't mean *we* have to," she argues, side eyeing me without actually looking at me. "I don't wanna know, and I'd rather not have those images running around in my head, thank you very much."

The two of them move along out of earshot and I bite down on the inside of my cheek, fighting a panic attack while I look around at the rest of the students in here.

I need Kade.

Abandoning the essay I'm working on, I shove my stuff into my bag and all but run for the door, keeping my head down while I walk the empty halls and make my way to his class. I won't be able to go in there with him, but I figure I can just stand right outside the door for forty minutes and wait for him to get out.

Feeling eyes on me from somewhere, I look over my shoulder just as I round the corner, squealing before I can stop it when I bounce right into someone.

"Why so jumpy?" Jasper asks, catching me by my elbows to back me up the way I came. "Wanna go for a walk?"

"Get the fuck away from m—"

"Shh," he whispers, lifting a silver blade to my lips. "I know you like to scream, but I wouldn't make too much noise if I were you."

My heart beats out of control and I run around him without thinking, desperate to get to Kade, locking my jaw when he fists my hair and pulls my chest to his.

"You know you dropped this in the church the other night, right?" he asks, shaking his head at me as he moves the knife down to my throat. "I'm a little sad I missed the show, but tell me something, Nicky," he goes on, teasing my flesh with the razor sharp edge. "Does your brother fuck like he fights? Because—"

"What have you done?" I choke out, unable to hide the terror in my eyes. "What did you tell them?"

"Sweetie, please, don't get upset," he says softly. "I didn't say anything about you and Kade and I won't."

"But we're not even—"

"Of course you're not," he cuts in, chuckling to himself while he continues walking me backwards. "Because Kade wouldn't even *dream* of touching another boy, would he? He hates gays just like your daddy does, and now he hates you, too." He feigns a pout, leaning in to speak over my lips. "*That's* what I told them."

"Why... why would you *do* that?"

"*Why?*" he echoes, his pale eyes darkening with something that looks like rage. "Your brother beat the shit out of me just for *touching* you and you're asking me *why*? Are you fucking stupid?"

I keep my mouth shut and he grits his teeth, turning on me to shove me up into the lockers. Wincing at the pain in my back, I hold my breath and keep my head as still as possible, fucking terrified he's about to cut me open with the knife he's pushing against my throat.

"Wanna go for a walk?" he asks again, his tone switching from mad to teasing.

"What are you talking about?"

"Well, I'm so glad you asked," he says dramatically, smirking when he catches the mixture of confusion and fear on my face. "I'm gonna drug you and take you out to the football field, nice and private, then I'm gonna pin you down beneath the bleachers and put my dick in your ass," he explains, shrugging as if that's a completely normal thing to say to someone. "I haven't decided if I want you on your back or your knees yet, but we'll sort that out when we get there."

"Jas…" I try, but he ignores me, running his free hand over my back to dip his fingers beneath my jeans.

"Then I'm gonna take a few pictures of you getting fucked by a boy, keeping my face out of the shot, because, you know, *gay haters* and all that, and—fuck me, do you *shave*?" he groans, roughly shoving his dry finger into my hole, yanking me into him until my chest bumps his. "God, I can't wait to get in here."

My tears fall freely and I fight a sob, knowing I can't move unless I want to die right here in this hallway.

"You wanna know the best part?" he asks, using the tip of the blade to draw a line on my cheek. "As soon as I send my new pictures to everyone in town, they're gonna be lining up to skin your ass alive. They'll probably kill you, won't they? *You'll* be the one in the ground and Kade'll lose his fucking mind without you, piece by piece until there's nothing left of it. *That's* his punishment for pissing me off."

"He'll find you first," I breathe out, wincing at the burning pain in my ass. "Don't you get that? You might be able to do whatever you want to me with that knife in your hand but you're already a dead boy walking."

He hums like he doesn't give a fuck and rips his finger out, shoving his hand into his back pocket to lift a white pill to my mouth. "Open up for me, sweetie."

No drugs unless they come from me.

I squeeze my lips together and he glares, forcing his fingers into my mouth to pry my teeth open. I take a risk and try to bite him, but then a few familiar voices fill my ears and he clicks his tongue.

"No fun," he complains, quickly spinning me

around to trade places with me, fisting my hoodie to keep me close as he leans back against the lockers. "I really did want to show your brother a picture of my cum leaking out of your sexy hole, but we're gonna have to skip the good bits and get straight to the last part."

"What the hell are y—"

"Dude, get off me!" he shouts, shoving me back as hard as he can. "Are you outta your fucking mind?"

"What are you two doing?" Mark asks, snatching my collar when I dip my head to try and get around them.

Fuck.

"He just tried to shove his tongue down my throat," Jasper lies, hiding the knife behind his back while he spits on the floor at my feet. "You're fucking sick, man."

"What the fuck, Nicky?" Austin frowns, pulling his head back in disgust. "Are you really a fag?"

"No—"

"Bullshit," Mark bites out, sneering at me while he pushes me towards Parker. "If the rumors aren't true why do you look so fucking scared right now?"

"I'm *not,*" I tell him, but my voice is shaking and so are my hands, my face soaked with tears while they trap me in the middle of their human circle. "Kade…"

Nodding at each other, they walk towards me and I scramble to pull my phone from my pocket, sobbing for real this time when I realize it's not there.

How is it not fucking there?

Just then, footsteps echo at the end of the hall and the four of them move as one, pulling on my clothes while they shove my head into the locker room door. It opens at the force of it and I trip over one of their feet, but I don't fall because they're holding me up, dragging me to the row of showers in the corner.

"Let go of me," I growl, kicking my legs out with my arms twisted up behind my back. "Let go!"

They don't let go.

My nostrils flare and I fight like fuck to get away from them, but they're stronger than me and we all know it.

It's finally happening.

My brother's worst nightmare is coming to life and there's nothing I can do to stop it.

"Did you really think we were gonna let this shit go when you've watched us get naked in here?" one of them hisses, but I can't tell which one he is when they're all talking at once, making me dizzy while they toss me back and forth between them.

"Which one of us do you wanna fuck the most, huh?"

"I bet it's Parker."

"It better not be me," Parker throws back, smashing his elbow into my jaw before he kicks me to the floor. "My dad's gonna kill me when he finds out I've been friends with a faggot my whole life, you disgusting little shit."

My nose cracks against the tiles and I try to scream, but all I can do is gag on the blood in my mouth, struggling to breathe with this blinding pain tearing through my skull. I spit one of my back teeth out and lift my shoulders up to my ears, instinctively protecting my head while they kick me in my ribs, my back, my face, so hard that I can feel my bones breaking, my flesh being torn open by their bare hands and feet. Still tearing at my clothes, they make fun of my scars and sneer at the purple marks all over my body, beating me even harder when Jasper points out that they're hickeys, not bruises.

"Kade…"

"*Kade*," someone mocks, pulling my hair to hit me in the face, over and over again until it's wet with blood and spit. "Your brother doesn't give a shit about you anymore, dipshit. If anything, he'll *thank* us for doing this *for* him. You're *nothing* to him, Nicky."

I almost laugh at that, but I don't.

I *can't*.

He eventually drops my head and my eyes begin to fade at the edges, seeing nothing but dark, blurry shapes moving about around me. I throw up without moving a muscle and rest my cheek against the dirty drain, wishing I could speak so I could beg them to hurry up and get it over with.

It hurts too fucking much, and I'd rather die.

I'd rather feel *nothing*.

I don't feel nothing, though.

I feel every excruciating second of being beaten to death, and the last thing I see before I finally get my wish is Jasper standing in the corner, winking at me while he sucks on the middle finger he had in my ass.

I hope he dies, too.

CHAPTER 21
KADE

THE BELL RINGS and I stand from my seat at the back of the room, walking out to the hall by myself considering Mark and the boys skipped out to smoke a joint about a half hour ago. Ignoring all the students milling about between classes, I make my way to the library to check on Nicky before I have to leave him again. He's not at any of the round tables where he usually sits to study, so I keep going and check the aisles, gritting my teeth when I realize he's not in here.

This little brat.

Knowing he's hiding from me, I drag a hand over my mouth and take my phone out to call him, pulling my head back in anger when the fucker sends me to voicemail. I'm just about to call him again, but then a text comes through and I stop walking to read it.

Nicky: Can't answer. I'm in the library.

I frown at that, looking around again before I text him back.

Kade: Upstairs?

Nicky: Yep.

I let out a sigh and head up to the upper level, finding him sitting at a table with his back to me, his black hood pulled over his head while he writes away in his notebook. I smile to myself and walk over to him, leaning over his shoulder to rest my hand on the back of his chair.

"You're not funny," I whisper in his ear, pulling his hood down to run my fingers through his hair.

Only his hair isn't black, and that's not fucking Nicky.

Jasper tips his head back on my chest and I quickly get out from behind him, scrunching my nose when I catch the stupid smirk on his face.

"What the fuck are you doing?" I grit out, looking around again to search for my brother.

"Homework," he says simply, making a show of rolling his eyes as if *I'm* the idiot here.

"Where's Nicky?"

"Last time I saw him was in the shower," he informs me, groaning quietly while he pulls on his dick through his jeans. "He was so fucking tight and *soft*, man. Do you think he shaves his hole or is it naturally that hairle—"

Before he can finish, I grab the back of his neck and smash his cheek into the table, my nostrils flaring with the effort it's taking not to throw him across this fucking room. I know he's a lying bitch, but still…

"I'm gonna kill you."

"Is that so?" he mumbles against the wood, laughing

at me as if he thinks I'm joking. "Right here in front of all those people downstairs? That's awfully bold of you."

I growl and let him go, ripping my hands through my hair while I look over the railing above the floor below.

Something's not right.

Nicky's not here.

But he *told* me he was here…

Just as I think it, my eyes widen and I spin around to look at Jasper, grabbing him again to search his jeans for Nicky's phone. I throw him down on his back and pull it out from his pocket, locking my jaw when I find the silver knife I gave to Nicky the other night.

No…

Jasper grins happily and opens his mouth to say something, but he doesn't get the chance before I take him by his throat and slam his head down on the table.

"Tell me where he is."

"I already told y—"

"Where the *fuck* is my brother?!" I shout, my right hand shaking as I push the tip of the blade into his jaw.

"Dead," he manages to say, struggling to breathe with my fingers digging into his neck. "Better hurry if you wanna see his body before they take it to the morgue."

All the color drains from my face and I move as fast as I can, knocking into people while I rush out through the library and into the hallway. Blind rage and cold fear consume me as I check every bathroom, every janitors closet, every fucking stairwell I pass, but I can't find him.

I can't fucking find him.

"Where are you, baby?" I whisper, my heart lodged in my throat while I think about what Jasper said.

Dead.

His *body.*

Last time I saw him was in the shower…

"Kade, what are you doing?" Arianna asks, squealing when I shove past her and take off running. "Kade!"

I get to the boys locker room within seconds and push my way inside, almost slipping on the water beneath my feet while I head straight for the showers.

That's not water, Kade…

I finally get to where I need to be and stop dead in my tracks, because the scene in front of me is something taken right out of the horrors that haunt me in my sleep.

The first thing I see is my baby brother lying face down on the floor beneath a downpour of icy cold water.

And the second thing I see is blood.

So much fucking blood.

I choke on my own saliva and fall to my knees beside him, reaching up to shut the shower off before I gently roll him over onto his side. The sight of his beaten face makes me choke some more and I tear my jacket off, frantically pulling my phone from my pocket while I wrap it around his freezing cold body.

"Don't you dare be dead," I cry, shielding his form with mine while I press two fingers to his pulse. "Don't be dead, don't be dead, *please,* don't be dea—"

"What the hell is going on in h… oh my god."

I whip my head over my shoulder to find our old gym teacher standing behind me, his eyes wide in horror as he takes in the state of Nicky's unmoving body.

"Nine one one, what's your emergency?"

"Talk to them," I rush out, tossing my phone into his fumbling hands. "Tell them he's not breathing."

He looks down at it and hesitates as if he's unsure, and I swear to god if my brother wasn't in this state right now I'd get up and cut his fucking throat out.

"Talk to them!"

He jumps at my tone and does as he's told, quickly pressing the speakerphone button before he tells them what's happening. I turn my attention back to Nicky and follow their instructions word for word, double checking his pulse again while I roll him to his back.

"I don't feel anything," I rasp, my features screwed up with pain I never thought possible when he just lies there with his mouth hanging open.

"You're sure?"

"Yes, I'm fucking sure."

"Okay, give him CPR," the woman on the phone says to me. "Thirty chest compressions and two breaths. The other one of you needs to keep your fingers on his pulse and tell me if his heart starts beating again."

I nod and do exactly as she says, pressing my hands to his chest to try and bring him back to life.

"Come on, baby," I plead, my own heart pumping wildly against my rib cage. *"Wake up."*

He doesn't wake up, but I don't stop trying, begging him not to leave me because I can't fucking do this.

If he's really gone, I will kill myself as soon as I'm done with Jasper and I won't think twice about it.

He thinks he's below me—that he's my annoying little shadow or some shit—but he couldn't be more wrong.

I'm *his* shadow.

I follow him around and keep him close because I can't *not* be around him.

I can't fucking live without him.

"*Nicky*," I growl, banging my fist into his chest, a little harder than I meant to. "I said *wake up!*"

He chokes on the water in his mouth and I release a broken cry, leaning over him with one hand on the tile next to his shoulder. And then I laugh for some reason, my emotions fighting for control while I wipe my face with the back of my arm. His beautiful eyes open and I help him turn his head to the side, carefully holding it up for him while he throws up all over the floor. He gags and begins shivering uncontrollably, clutching my wrist while he winces like he's in agony.

"Kade," he whimpers, but I don't think he can see me.

"I got you," I say quietly, my voice cracking as my tears fall down to his face. "I'm here, baby. I got you."

Twenty seven minutes.

It took the paramedics *twenty seven* fucking *minutes* to get to him, then another eighteen minutes in the locker room, then another nine minutes to carry him out to the ambulance and drive us to the hospital. That was fifty four minutes total since I found him dead, and I spent the next ninety two minutes after that glaring at the old ass bitch of a nurse who said I had to sit in the waiting room with all the other patients' families.

I didn't sit.

I paced the floor in front of thirty one other people and fantasized about wrapping my hands around her wrinkled neck, squeezing the life out of her body until her slimy little tongue fell out of her mouth.

Fuck me, I'm going crazy.

Trying and failing to calm myself down, I rest my elbows on the edge of Nicky's bed and gently hold his knuckles to my lips, once again counting the seconds ticking by while I stare at his sleeping form.

Counting is helping.

Counting things keeps my mind busy, away from the guilt eating away at me and trying to swallow me whole. But even still, every time I look at his swollen face, all I can see is the thick streaks of blood coating the walls, the cold shower raining down on him, the way he would have cried for me while they were beating him black and blue…

God fucking damn it.

My breathing picks up and I smash my fist into my face, hating myself because I should have done better.

I should have *realized sooner*.

I should have fucking *been* there for him the way I've been promising since we were tiny little kids.

"I'm sorry," I whisper, slowly taking his hand again

to lift it back to my lips. "God, baby, I'm so fucking sorry."

His eyes remain closed and I grind my teeth together, looking up when the nurse who comes to check on him every thirty minutes walks inside. This one's younger and a lot hotter than the one from the waiting room, but she's still a nasty little bitch all the same.

"How long until he wakes up?" I ask again, watching her every move while she checks his blood pressure on the monitor next to his head.

"How long's a piece of string?" she throws back, flicking the blanket away to look at the stitches on his side.

My nostrils flare and I wait very patiently for her to finish, then I carefully pull it back up to his chest and tuck it back in to keep him warm. "Is he in pain?"

"I'm sure he's fine, Kade," she sighs, snatching the clipboard from the end of the bed to write something on it. "He's got a mild concussion, a little broken nose, a couple fractured ribs and some minor cuts and bruises. There's no internal bleeding and his vitals are good. It's really not the end of the world, you know?"

I inhale a long breath and force it out slowly, struggling to fight my father's temper while I stare at the side of her face. I could stand up and scare the ever loving shit out of her if I wanted to, but I don't do that. I will not lose my shit in this hospital, because if I lose my shit, they'll call security to throw me out, and if they throw me out, Nicky won't have anyone to protect him.

I have to protect him.

I won't fail him again.

Never again.

She finally leaves the room and I look at Nicky, reaching up to move his bloody hair from his eyebrow, lightly brushing my thumb over the tube taped to his cheek. Three more minutes pass and I lose a little more of my sanity, allowing myself to seethe for a few seconds while I recount the stitches on his face. My hands are shaking again and I'm *vibrating* with rage, plotting and planning and picturing all the ways I could make that cunt suffer for what he did today.

But not just him.

There's too much blood on Nicky's skin, too many broken bones, too many goddamn *marks* on my boy's body for Jasper to have acted alone. He had to have had help, and even though Nicky's not awake to give me their names, I already know exactly where we're headed when I get him back on his feet.

I saw the shock on their faces when I followed the paramedics to the ambulance in the parking lot, saw the fear in their eyes when they saw the look in mine.

I didn't say anything, because they already knew.

I'm gonna get every last one of them.

CHAPTER 22

NICKY

I'VE NEVER SEEN my brother cry.

Not once in… fifteen years.

He's always been the stronger one, but in this moment right here, as I slowly work my eyes open and find him sitting in a hospital room beside me, covered in blood from his face to his fingertips, he looks… weak.

He looks *broken*.

I move my knuckle over his lips and he looks up, eyes wide as he bounces them between mine. I frown at him and he lets out a noise I've never heard before, his shoulders visibly shaking while he drops his forehead to my arm. My heart aches in my chest and I try to lift the hand that isn't wrapped up between his, weakly moving it over to run it through his hair.

"It's okay," I rasp out, unable to speak properly because my throat is too dry. "You got me, you son of a bitch."

He laughs against me and I frown again, stopping

when I realize that's what's hurting the front of my skull. He stays like that for I don't know how long—just a few seconds, probably—then he moves closer and grabs a plastic cup of water from somewhere, careful not to lean on me while he holds it up to my mouth. I sip it without lifting my head and then turn my face towards him, watching him set it down on the side while I fight to swallow it. He watches me right back and I stare at his teary eyes, moving my finger to run it over the wetness covering his cheeks, then down to his lips.

"You're crying," I tell him, even though I'm sure he already knows that.

His features tighten and he makes that sound again, leaning over me to touch my forehead with his. "I thought I lost you, baby… I thought you *left* me."

"You'd never let me leave you."

He nods his agreement and I slide my hand around to the back of his neck, pulling him in until his mouth brushes mine. I kiss him and he lets me do it, taking over for me when my lips get too tired to move.

"Do you remember?" he asks, resting his forearms on the pillow either side of my head.

"Yeah."

"Does it hurt?"

"Yeah," I admit, wincing while I try to move my ass down a bit. "It really fucking hurts, Kade."

"Where?"

"Everywhere."

He growls quietly and reaches out to pick up some sort of button, but then something happens and he whips his head over his shoulder, flying off of me a second before our dad throws him back against the wall.

"*No,*" I try to scream, but all I end up doing is dry heaving, my chest and ribs tightening painfully while I watch him wrap his hands around my brother's throat.

"What the hell do you think you're doing?!"

"I wasn't *doing* anyth—"

"I saw you!" he roars, right up in his face while he yells so loud it makes my head throb. "I just watched you make out with your fucking brother, you sick cunt!"

Kade blinks at him and Dad punches the wall next to his head, making me jump, then he looks at me and glares like he'd rather see me dead, his lip curling as he moves his terrifying gaze over my form.

"You *deserved* this..." he accuses. "You're a fucki—"

"Officer Rivers?" a female voice asks, and I look over to find a pretty brunette nurse standing in the open doorway. "I'm sorry to interrupt, but there's another police officer here. He wants to talk to Nicky."

She doesn't even look at me when she says that, and any hope I had just now falls through the cracks, my silent tears slipping down to my ears when I realize she's not here to help us.

There's *no one* here to help us.

"That won't be necessary, my dear," Dad informs her, releasing Kade's neck to swipe his hands over the white button down he's wearing. "Take those tubes from my son's body and get the doctor to sign his discharge papers. Tell the officer I'll be out in a second."

She nods once and I shrink back as far as I can

manage, looking at Kade for help when she walks towards me.

"Wait a minute, this is bullshit!" he shouts, gritting his teeth at her while she takes my left arm and turns it over, making me wince as she slides the needle from my skin. "You can't just send him home like this."

She ignores him as if he doesn't exist and he mutters something I don't catch, ripping his hair out on both sides as he glances between me and her.

"Can you at least give him something for the pain?"

She looks at Dad and he shakes his head no, a nasty little snarl on his face while he throws some clean clothes at my chest. Kade catches them before they hit me and sets them down on the bed, taking two steps towards him when he takes one towards me.

"Get the fuck out," Kade says slowly, and even though I can't see his face, I can tell he looks vicious right now, fucking seething as he stares our father down.

The nurse leaves quietly but Dad remains still, his hands flexing at his sides while he looks between me and my brother. "You have ten minutes."

I release the breath I was holding and watch him step out into the hall, hiding my face behind my hands while I struggle not to fall apart. "Kade…"

"It's okay, Nicky," he assures me, but it's *not* okay and he should fucking *know* that.

"He's gonna kill us."

"He's not gonna kill us."

"Yes, he is!" I cry, gagging and choking on my own air, this burning pain inside me getting too much for me to handle. "Don't stand there and tell me he's not when you *know*… you know… I'm gonna be sick."

He moves quickly and I throw up into the cardboard bowl he's holding, my eyes watering while I clutch on to his wrists and let it all out. As soon as I'm finished, he gets rid of it and gently wipes my face with a wet paper towel, reaching over to feed me another couple sips of water. I rinse my mouth out and spit it back into the cup, breathing hard while I lean sideways against his body. The position hurts so much that it makes me sweat all over, but I need him too much to care.

"You okay?"

"No, I'm scared, Kade," I croak out, resting my sore cheek on his chest. "I don't wanna go with him."

"Baby, listen to me," he whispers, holding my head while he presses his mouth to my hair. "I don't want this either, but you have to know that I will *never* let him get you. I'll never let anyone get you like that again. I just need you to trust me, okay?"

I sniff and nod my head, hissing through my teeth when it causes my face to rub on his shirt. He tenses and pulls back a bit, studying the stitches there while he fists the hem of my hospital gown. He pulls it up slowly, and I can only imagine what he's seeing, his eyes darkening with rage as he moves them over my naked body. His hands start to shake and I think he's about to smash something, but then he shakes it off and moves to grab my clothes, scarily calm and collected while he stretches the collar of my t-shirt.

"I've got some pills stashed in my nightstand," he tells me, making sure to avoid my broken nose as he pulls it over my head. "Can you hang in there just a little bit longer?"

"How much longer?"

"Not much," he says vaguely, helping me the best he can while I try to get my arms through the holes. "Okay, get your ass to the edge of the bed and I'll do the rest."

I take another breath and do as I'm told, suddenly wishing I could just die again. My sweats are the hardest to put on, because my ribs are on fire and I can barely move without wanting to puke all over myself. He finally manages to get me dressed and then eases me up to my feet, holding me up by my hands while I wait for the room to stop spinning. I don't get to wait, though, because then our dad lets himself inside and crosses his arms over his chest, staring at us in disgust while he holds the door open with his back.

"Hurry up before I drag you myself."

Fuck, I hate him.

I move one foot in front of the other and Kade keeps me as close to his side as possible, making a point to stay between me and Dad as we walk out into the hall.

"Let go of his hand."

"Go fuck yourself."

His nostrils flare but he doesn't say anything else, probably because he doesn't want to cause a scene in front of all these people. I keep my head down and try to concentrate on walking, trying my hardest not to fall over at the way the floor keeps wobbling beneath me. My entire body throbs violently and I'm so spaced out that it's hard to think straight, but I don't miss the several pairs of eyes on us, the whispers following me and my brother as we make our way towards the exit.

They know.

They *all* know, and suddenly the nurse's nasty attitude makes a lot more sense than it did before.

"We weren't safe here, anyway, were we?"

"No," Kade says honestly, his voice quiet but cold.

I sneak a glance at him and find him seething again, his composure slipping while we walk out into the pouring rain. I whine into his side and he wraps his arm around my shoulder, covering me the best he can while he helps me into the back of Dad's cop car. He closes the door and rushes around to the other side, barely leaving me alone for a second before he's sliding into the seat beside me. Dad's eyes hit mine in the rear-view and I shiver in Kade's arms, but I don't bother asking him to turn the heat on. He wouldn't do it if I begged him to, so there's really no point wasting my breath.

The drive home is silent, and painful, and freezing, and even though Kade just told me I had to trust him, I can't help the pure terror rushing through me—the fear that these could be our last moments alive.

"Get out," Dad orders, pulling up behind the truck and ripping his keys from the ignition.

He jumps out of the driver's seat and waits for us to follow him, his impatience clear as he watches Kade help me. The rain is getting heavier now, soaking us from head to toe as we make our way up the narrow path. The three of us get inside and Dad slams the front door behind us, then he grabs Kade by his shoulders and shoves him into it head first. I let out a cry and lean my bruised back against the wall, barely able to keep myself standing as I watch him hit the floor.

"Kade, get up!" I shout, wishing I could do something to help him, wishing I wasn't so fucking weak, wishing a lot of things that'll probably never come true. *"Kade."*

His eyes soften for me and then he looks up at Dad, grinning for some reason despite the blood dripping from his temple. Dad growls through his teeth and chokes him with both hands, digging his thumbs into his throat while he rams his foot into his stomach. He does it again, and *again*, and Kade does *nothing*. Nothing but lie there and take it while our father beats the shit out of him, his ugly face turning red as he lays into him until he's out of breath. I flinch with every hit and wrap my arms around my stomach, furious with my brother because *what the fuck is he doing*?

Why isn't he fighting back?

"It's okay, Nicky," he reminds me, his voice raspy as he repeats the words he's told me so many times before. "Keep looking at me and pretend he's not here. It's just you and me, okay? No one but me."

No one but him.

I breathe fast and try to do as he says, holding his eyes while he takes another hit to the face, and another one, and then another five. It seems to go on forever, and I can't do this much longer.

I can't fucking *stand* this.

"Kade," I plead, but he doesn't do anything.

He lets himself get beat by the other man—the same one he told me to ignore—the same one who's been making our lives hell since the four of us became a family all those years ago.

"God, you make me sick," the man spits out, roughly hauling Kade up to his feet, his head whipping back and forth between the two of us. "Fucking disgusting, dirty little faggots. And *you*—"

I wince just as Kade pulls him back by his jacket, quickly ducking around him to block his path to me.

"Move."

"No."

"*Move* before I make you move."

"Fucking *try* it," Kade hisses, shoving him back with two hands on his chest, shoving him again as if he's proving some kind of point. "You can touch me all you want but that's only because I *allow* it. You touch my baby brother and I'll kill you right here."

"You'll *kill* me?" he echoes, shaking his head in amusement. "Boy, who the fuck do you think you're talking to? You think you can kill *me*?!"

"I think you're a pussy," Kade replies, stepping closer to crowd his space. "I *think* you beat the shit out of me and Mom because it made you feel like a big man. And I *think* you'll scream like a bitch when I finally get m—"

Dad lunges for him and Kade laughs like it's funny, looking at me over his shoulder while the bigger man lifts his hands up in surrender. I frown and try to make sense of what's happening, my eyes widening when I realize he's holding that silver knife to our dad's throat.

"How did you...?"

He winks at me and quickly tears Dad's jacket from

his shoulders, tossing it to my feet before he steals his phone, car keys, and both guns from his body. Dad's jaw ticks and he opens his mouth to say something, but he doesn't get the chance before Kade unlocks the door behind him—the one that leads to the small office just off the narrow hallway. Kade pushes him inside and knocks him off his feet, ignoring his shout while he rips the jeans from his thick legs. I scrunch my nose at that, confused as to what the hell he's doing, but he doesn't give me any type of clue as he pulls the door shut and fumbles with the key inside the lock. He twists it into place just as Dad bangs on it from the other side, trapped in there with no way to escape. There are no windows in that room—nothing he can use to get himself out. Just a few coats and shoes, some paperwork and an old computer that hasn't been switched on in years. Just as I think it, Kade rushes to the living room and rips the internet cable from the wall, grabbing a dining chair on his way back to shove it beneath the door handle.

"You think that'll stop him?" I ask hopefully, pressing my lips together when he lifts a finger to his mouth.

Shh.

I do as I'm told and he smirks like a maniac, slowly walking over to me to place his forearms on the wall either side of my head. I look up at him and take his bloody face in my hands, smirking right back at him when I finally catch that feral look in his dark blue eyes.

There he is.

CHAPTER 23

KADE

My little brother kisses me and I eagerly move my mouth against his, resisting the urge to squeeze him and wrap him up in my arms. I know it'll be a long time before I can do that again, and it only makes me more furious.

More hungry for revenge.

More desperate to find those stupid motherfuckers and make them pay for what they did to him.

Soon, I promise myself.

Soon, they'll be gone and Nicky will be safe.

I just have to stick to my plan.

"Drugs," I whisper into his mouth, remembering the most important part. "I'm gonna go up and get you some drugs, but I need you to tell me you're okay first. Please, just tell me you're not dying on me right now."

"I don't think I'm dying," he whispers back, frowning to himself while he moves his hands over my chest. "I mean, it kinda feels like it, actually, but I'm okay."

"You sure?"

He nods and I nod, too, leaning over to take our dad's guns from the pile of his things on the floor. I shove one into the back of my jeans and pull Nicky's sleeves down to his fingertips, reluctantly stepping away from him to place it between his tiny hands. I know I told him I'd never give him one of these, because I'm terrified he'll fuck up and hurt himself by accident, but desperate times and all that.

"Point it at the door and shoot him in the face if he gets out," I say quietly, showing him how to hold it with his finger ready on the trigger. "Don't stop until he's dead."

"But… he's not gonna get out, right?"

"No," I assure him. "He's not getting out."

"Kade, wait."

"What?"

"Are *you* okay?" he asks me, scanning the damage on my face. "You're bleeding."

"I'm fine, Nicky," I say honestly, because I can barely feel it with all this adrenaline pumping through me.

He lets out a breath and I turn around to head for the stairs, fucking hating myself for leaving him there all by himself, but I don't have enough time to get him all the way up here and back down again. Moving as quickly as I can, I grab the little bag of pills from my nightstand and snatch my speaker from the side, then I open my closet and dig out the black ski mask and the old burner phone I stashed in the bottom corner. I shove those into my pocket and move across the hall to our dad's room, careful not to leave any fingerprints behind while I steal a pair of black gloves from his dresser. I don't think it'll come to that after what I'm about to do on his behalf, but I can't be too careful.

I can't go to jail and leave Nicky alone out here.

I just *can't.*

As soon as I have everything I need, I head back out to the hall and rush downstairs, relieved when I find him standing exactly where I left him. He looks at me and lowers the gun to his side, tipping his head back against the wall while he waits for me to come for him. I do and he sticks his tongue out as far as he can, smiling a little bit as I drop one of the pink pills on top.

"Good boy," I praise, watching his throat move as he swallows it. "You remember what these do to you?"

"Make me hard as a motherfucker," he mutters, reaching down to adjust his dick in his sweats.

I laugh lightly at that, carefully batting his hand away to do it for him. "Yeah, well, if it gets really bad, I'll suck the cum out of it later," I tell him, enjoying the needy little groan he lets out despite the pain he's in.

"That was mean."

"Baby, you haven't seen *mean*," I tease, pulling back to set the speaker down on the table by the front door.

Annoyed by the threatening shouts and curses coming from the office on my left, I connect my phone and turn the volume up to drown him out, thankful the neighbors are used to us blaring our music into the early hours of the morning. Nicky winces and lifts his hands up to his ears, making me feel like an even bigger asshole than I already am. I take Dad's things from the floor and lead him through to the living room, wrapping a throw blanket around his shoulders before I set him down on the couch. He leans back and frowns again, but he doesn't ask me any questions as he watches me light the fire opposite him. It's only a small one—nothing like the one we have up at our mother's cabin—but it'll do just fine for what we need it for.

Keeping one eye on Nicky and the other on the office door, I walk through to the kitchen and take the burner phone from my pocket, my heart racing in my chest while I dial the number and click the call button.

I don't trust this crazy son of a bitch—because I don't trust anyone but my brother—but I'm fresh out of options here and I need him more than I care to admit.

"You little pricks, I told you not to call me this late," he hisses, probably hiding somewhere in his cell considering they're not allowed phones in prison.

"I'm moving up the plan."

"To when?"

"Tonight," I answer, using my free hand to pull my dad's jeans over the top of mine. "Right now, actually."

"Oh, really?" he asks, pausing for a few seconds before he speaks again. "Do you mind telling me wh—"

"They attacked Nicky, Pres," I choke out, furious with these fucking tears that won't stop leaking from my eyes. "They *got* him and I wasn't fucking *there* and —"

"Wait, who got him?"

"Mark and Parker and Austin and fucking *Jasper*," I growl, knowing he has absolutely no clue who I'm talking about. "He's never done *anything* to them and they killed him in the locker room at school. They just fucking *left* him there. And my dad..." I laugh, but it sounds strange to my own ears. "You know what my dad said when he saw his own son lying in a hospital bed, covered from head to toe in their marks and bruises? You *deserved* this..." I repeat his words, grinding my teeth so hard it hurts. "I want him dead."

"Okay. Kade, maybe you should think ab—"

"I don't have time to *think*," I stress, squeezing my eyes shut while I pull the hair from my scalp. "I can't... fuck, I'm losing my mind. They *know* and they could come for us any second now and I'm not fucking *ready*."

"Dude, you're not making any sense."

"I'm fucking Nicky," I blurt out, stopping where I stand to look at him, his tiny little body wrapped up in the blanket with his shoulders hunched up to his ears. "I fuck him all the time and he *loves* it. *I* love it. And I love him, too. I think I always have..."

"Jesus Christ," my uncle mutters, clearly disgusted over what I just told him. "Please, tell me that's a joke."

"It's not."

"Fuck me, are you *crazy*? What the hell is the matter with you? He's your little brother, you dirty—"

"You better make it hurt, man," I warn, lying through my teeth in an attempt to scare him. "You better make him beg or we'll come in there and we'll make *you* beg."

"Kade—"

I hang up and smash the phone into the sink, taking it out just as quickly when I realize I can't leave it there.

I pull air in through my nostrils and grab the jacket my dad was wearing before, throwing it on over my clothes to make myself look a little bigger than I am. I zip it up to my neck and pull the hood over my head, then I put his shoes on and walk back to the living room, freezing mid step when I catch the look on my brother's face.

"Nicky—"

"You're going after the boys, aren't you?" he accuses, glaring at me as if he thinks I'm betraying him, his breathing quickening as he launches himself into a panic attack. "You're *leaving* me here with h—"

"*No*," I growl, dropping to my knees at his feet, taking his hands to lift them up to my neck. "Baby, I'm taking you with me. You're coming and I'm gonna let you watch me hurt them like they hurt you."

He blinks at that, swallowing while he moves his eyes over my face. "What if you get caught?"

"I'm not getting caught."

"Why did you let him beat you?"

Because if you hurt, I hurt.

"Because I need the bruises for later."

"What's happening later?" he asks, but then the clever fucker figures it out and he blinks again, his white flesh paling even more with fear and disbelief. "Kade..."

"I won't let anything happen to us," I promise, gently pulling him up to his feet, shaking my head when he opens his mouth to argue with me. "I know you're in pain, and I know this isn't how it was supposed to happen, but it's now or never, Nicky. It's —"

"Now," he says clearly. "I choose now."

Decision made, I release another breath and bring him back towards the entryway, letting go of his hands to pull the gloves and mask from my pocket. I kiss him one more time and then quickly pull them on, satisfied when I realize he's still got the other gun in his pocket. *Throne* by Bring Me The Horizon plays loudly through the speaker on the table and I turn it up even more, leaving it there before I walk him outside and lock the front door behind us.

"Keep your head down," I whisper, pulling his hood over his nose to ensure his face stays hidden.

He does as he's told and I walk him out to the street, hidden by the thick trees on both sides as well as the lack of lights out here. Passing the truck Dad must have picked up from school at some point today, I get my brother into the passenger seat of the cop car and then walk around to the driver's side, quickly starting the ignition to pull off towards where we're going. I turn the radio off and whip the heat up as high as it goes, glancing at the clock on the dash to check the time.

It takes six minutes to get there from here, which is both too much and not enough all at once.

"Baby, tell me," I rasp, curling my gloved fingers around the steering wheel. "Tell me what they did to you."

He hesitates, anxiously playing with his cuticles while he makes himself even smaller. "All of it?"

"All of it," I insist, and he shudders, his eyes closing while he relives the torment he went through today.

I don't want to do this to him, but I need to hear it

before we get there, and I need him *not* to let this nightmare eat away at him every day for the rest of his life. If he tells me, maybe I can take some of the pain from him, and I can carry it with me until the day I die.

Ten long seconds of silence follow, stretching in the small amount of space between us, and then he tells me everything—everything that happened from the minute those girls were talking shit in the library to the minute they had him on the floor in the showers.

He tells me about Jasper, and I wish I had more time on the clock, more minutes to make him scream for every second he made my brother feel weak and helpless and *alone…*

"Kade," Nicky says quietly, and I don't miss the shake in his voice, the fear in his eyes when he catches the black rage in mine. "Are you mad at me?"

Fucking hell.

I pull up onto Mark's huge driveway and shove the car into park, leaving the headlights on while I lean over until our foreheads are almost touching. "I *love* you, you idiot," I grit out, stressing each word to ensure he hears me loud and clear. "I'm so fucking *mad* I can't see straight, but it's not *at* you. It's *for* you. Every fucking thing I do and every move I make is *for you*. Okay?"

"Okay."

"Okay," I repeat, breathing hard against the inside of my mask. "I'll be back for you in two minutes. Count them."

"Huh?"

"It helps," I explain, and then I'm moving, climbing out of the car to make my way up to the front door.

It swings open before I have the chance to knock politely, and Mark's mom smiles at me, fake as shit and scared for her son, I'm assuming. "Officer Rivers," she says sweetly, lifting her hands up when I don't stop walking towards her. "Look... I know why you're here, but he didn't do it. He would *never* do such a thi—"

I quickly slap my palm over her mouth and hold the back of her neck with my free hand, blocking her view of Nicky while I force her back into her own house. She squeals and wraps her fingers around my forearm, mumbling something useless and unimportant while I drag her through to the kitchen. Avoiding her eyes, I keep my head low and shove her into a dining chair, taking my dad's handcuffs from his jacket to secure her wrists behind her back. She struggles and keeps talking, but I don't hear what she's saying as I search for something to blindfold her with.

Forty eight...

Forty nine...

Knowing the boys could walk in on me any second now, I check my brother through the window and grab what I need from the island, the chair scraping her expensive wooden floors as I spin her to face the corner.

"Eric, please," she begs, using my father's first name to scratch at his humanity. "Please, don't hurt my baby."

Your baby hurt mine.

But of course I can't say that to her.

"Your baby knows too much," I whisper instead, keeping my voice low to ensure she can't tell it's me, ignoring her cries while I gag her with a hand towel.

"*No—*"

I shove the fabric down to the back of her throat and steal the scarf from her neck, covering her eyes with it to ensure she can't see. I triple knot it at the back of her head—which takes me fifteen seconds too long because she won't stop fucking moving—then I leave her there and head back out to the car.

"You're twenty one seconds late," Nicky informs me, feigning a pout while I help him up to his feet.

I breathe a laugh and shake my head at him, my pulse hammering against the side of my neck while I lead him to the front door. The two of us walk through the house in silence, nothing but the sound of the quiet, muffled noises coming from the kitchen as we make our way to the patio doors on the back wall. Nicky side eyes me, but he doesn't say anything as he follows me out into the rain, his pupils blown thanks to the drugs running through his system. Our feet hit the decking and I stop him with a light touch to his abs, smirking to myself when the scent of cigarettes and weed hits my nostrils.

As sad as it is, the fact that the cops don't give a fuck about a gay boy being beaten to death actually works in my favor. These bastards aren't in jail for what they did this morning. They're not even being questioned for it. Instead they're here, right where I knew they'd be because I know how they think. Parker and Austin spend almost every night at this massive house, anyway. And Jasper… I'm betting he's only with them because they've forced him to be here, threatened him to go along with whatever plan they have to get rid of me.

The thought brings another smirk to my lips.

Nicky moves beside me and I slide my eyes down to his, slowly guiding him back against the wall where I'll be able to see him at all times.

"Don't move," I mouth, tilting my head down to the gun in his pocket. "Same thing as before. If one of them gets around me, you shoot until they're on the ground."

He nods his obedience and I walk away, making a quick stop at the fully stocked shed on my left. I grab Mark's favorite baseball bat from its space in the corner, flip it around in my hand, and walk to the wooden canopy at the end of the yard. Their hushed voices get clearer as I get closer, but they soon stop altogether when they realize someone's coming from behind. Parker spots me first and immediately tries to make a run for it, but he doesn't get far before I smash the bat into the side of his face, knocking him back down to the cushioned couch with one hard hit. Mark looks from me to Nicky and I go for him next, hitting the brave fucker in the nose when he turns like he's about to take a swing at me. I hit him again and then do the same with Austin, snatching Jasper's white hair from behind the same way he did with Nicky earlier.

"*Fuck*! Kad—"

I pull the scrawny little bitch backwards and shove him down to the ground, enjoying the flash of fear in his eyes as I swing the bat down to his stomach. The rain soaks my face through my mask and makes it hard to see what I'm doing, but I don't stop.

I don't talk.

I don't make a fucking sound.

I just break every bone within my reach.

Every nose, every rib, every kneecap…

I beat them until they're the same color as the boy standing behind me, making their bodies shake and bleed until their pain-filled screams fill my baby brother's ears.

It's not enough.

It'll *never* be enough, but I don't have time for more.

As soon as I've got all four of them crumpled up on the gravel, I smash the bat into their skulls one after the other, starting with Mark, then Parker, then Austin, and then I get to Jasper. He drags himself along the grass on his stomach, somehow still moving despite the fact I've broken both of his legs in four places. I walk around him and kick him over onto his back, cocking my head while I look down at his bloody face.

"You're obsessed," I point out, unsure whether it's with me or Nicky or both of us, but it doesn't really matter now. "You're crazy, aren't you?"

"So what if I am?" he taunts me, trying for a grin as he looks upside down toward the deck. "I thought Nicky liked crazy boys."

My nostrils flare and I kick him in the face, leaning over to lift his head off the ground and pull his eyes back to mine. "Why did you move here?"

"Not f-for you," he stammers, his body shaking with a choked out laugh. "Honestly, Kade, not everything is about you and your stupid little brother, you know? I moved here because h-he forced me to."

"What the fuck are you talking about?"

"He's that gay teacher's son," Nicky guesses, still leaning back against the wall by the doors, speaking quietly to ensure Mark's mom doesn't hear. "The one Dad was talking about right before he showed up the next day. Your dad got fired when they found out he was gay, right?" he asks Jasper. "Then everyone at school probably turned on you, too, so you had to change your names and move here."

"Great choice of town, I know," Jasper says dryly, breathing heavily while he stares up at the sky. "I'm not that mad about it, though. The guys at my old school weren't half as hot as y—"

I drop his head and stand up to my full height, pulling the gun from my pocket to shoot him in the face. Nicky sucks in a breath and the woman inside screams loud enough for us to hear it, meaning it's time for us to go. I empty three more bullets into the other three faces beneath me, then I drop the bat on the ground and walk back up to Nicky.

"What the fuck did you just do?!" he whisper yells, his eyes wide with shock and horror while he studies the mess I've made in front of him.

"No one touches you," I remind him, leaving it at that while I pull the patio door open.

I tilt my head for him to follow me and he does, swallowing a few times while we make our way back to the car. I don't help him this time, because I'm caked in blood and I can't get any on him, but he manages to climb in by himself without touching anything with his fingers. I jump in beside him and reverse out of the driveway, the tires screeching beneath us while I speed off through the gate. A flash of headlights blinds me for a second and I look over, cursing when I realize it's

Mark's dad. I thought he was out of town for a week, but he must have come back early after finding out about Nicky. I react without thinking and swerve into the side of his car, hoping that'll distract him for a minute or two before he goes inside.

I just need a minute or two.

Nicky winces and I lock my jaw, resisting the urge to reach over and comfort him. "You okay?"

"No, you fucker," he breathes out, his sleeve pressed to his mouth as if he's trying his hardest not to puke. "I can't believe you just did that. You *killed* them."

"They killed you," I reason, quickly looking both ways before I run the red light in front of me.

"Jesus Christ, Kade, haven't you ever heard of two wrongs don't make a right?"

"I have, and I think it's bullshit."

He laughs at that, but I don't think he finds me funny. "You're out of your fucking mind."

I shrug and break every speed limit there is, almost crashing into the back of my truck as I force the car up onto our tiny front lawn. "Shit, I'm sorry, baby."

"Are you talking to me or your truck?"

"My truck doesn't give me attitude," I joke, climbing out to walk around to him.

He shakes his head at me and damn near falls out of the car, his walk a little shorter this time considering the passenger side is right next to the front door. I follow in behind him and pull the ski mask from my face, careful not to get any of the dead boys' blood on my skin as I throw it into the fire.

"*Boys!*" Dad roars over the music, but I don't even

look his way, quickly ripping his gloves and clothes from my body to burn those, too. "Open this fucking door!"

"Fuck, he's breaking it, Kade."

"I'm almost done."

"*Kade.*"

"*I'm almost done,*" I repeat, quickly tossing any evidence they can tie to us, dropping both guns into the kitchen sink before I rush back over to Nicky. "Let him come for me and then get inside the office."

"What?"

"I'm gonna kill both of you!" Dad threatens, his voice getting louder as he manages to split the wood.

"I need you to make it look like he locked us up in there," I explain, feeding him another pill as I back him up into the hall. "Can you do that for me?"

He nods and I slide my middle finger over his tongue, kissing the nasty cut on his bottom lip before I move him out of the way. I unlock the office door with the sleeve of my jacket and Dad runs out dressed in nothing but his shirt and underwear, which would be a little funny if he wasn't shoving his fist into my face. He punches me and I purposely fall back a few steps, glaring at him while I spit the blood from my mouth. He keeps coming for me and I keep moving backwards, relieved when Nicky stumbles into the office like I told him to.

Good boy.

"I'm gonna kill both of you," Dad says again, and I nod mockingly, fighting a grin when he backhands me in the jaw to stop me. "You think this is funny?!"

"I already told you what I think, asshole."

He growls and takes a fist full of my hair, hitting me so hard that I fall down for real this time, my temples throbbing while he pins me to the carpet. Seconds turn to minutes and I do everything I can to keep his attention on me, laughing to myself when I catch the blue and red lights flashing across the ceiling.

Fucking figures three straight guys and a closeted gay boy get themselves killed and the cops come running to catch the bad guy.

Dad's body tenses above mine and he stops punching me, his eyes widening when it hits him. "What—"

"You *deserve* this," I tell him, just as the front door gets kicked open and bangs against the wall.

The police run in shouting and Veronica lifts her gun to his head—the same blonde chick who tried to talk to me and Nicky the night our mom was killed.

"Get on your knees!"

"Ronnie…"

"Get on your knees!" she screams again, but he doesn't get the chance to do as he's told before one of the cops tackles him off of me, cracking my dad's head on the corner of the coffee table as they both go down together. "Goddamnit."

"You fucking bastard!" the guy cries in his face, making me grin on the inside when I realize that's his own partner—a massive bald dude who just so happens to be Mark's uncle. "He was my nephew, you son of a bitch! My little sister's fucking kid!"

"Someone get him out of here!" Veronica seethes,

snatching a blue glove from her pocket to hit the stop button on my speaker. "Jesus Christ, that's awful."

Two of the other cops haul him up by his arms and Veronica tilts her chin for me to get out of the way, still holding her gun to my dad's head as she carefully walks towards him. I keep my head down and move for the office to get back to Nicky, steadying myself with my hands on the doorframe, my erratic heart leaping up to my throat when I catch the look in his eyes.

"Baby, come here."

He launches himself at me and I wrap my arm around his waist, holding his head with my free hand while he drops his face to my chest. He shakes against me with his fingers curled around the front of my jacket, and I don't have to look at his eyes to know his tears aren't fake. He's not putting it on for the cops. He's just sad and relieved and hurting all at once.

I turn us around and lean back against the wall in the hallway, watching the police as they find the clothes burning on the shitty fire, the murder weapon in the sink and the bloody shoes just outside the back door. They cuff our dad's hands behind his back and he snarls at us as he passes, his nasty eyes roaming our bodies pressed together as they drag him out of the house we grew up in.

"It's over, baby brother," I whisper, gently brushing my mouth over his ear. "He's gone."

"Are you sure?"

"Positive," I answer, moving down to kiss the crook of his neck. "He's gone and he's never coming back."

CHAPTER 24

NICKY

THERE's no music in my ears.

Kade set my head down on his lap a little while ago and put his headphones in for me, but there's nothing playing, probably because he doesn't want to make my headache any worse than it already is, but wants to make it look like I can't hear them at the same time.

Because at least if I can't hear them, I can't answer any of their annoying questions.

Questions that make me nervous as fuck.

I think they believed the story we made up and the lies Kade told them, but they've been here for ages, taking photos and bagging evidence and…

Fuck me, this burns.

I wince before I can stop it and Kade glares, hitting the paramedic with a look that says *hurry up or die.*

I popped the stitches on my face at some point between the hospital and here, and Veronica *insisted* she needed to have us both checked out before she could leave us alone. I still can't tell whether she's a good person or not, but she looks at us like she cares and it reminds me of Mom.

I miss my fucking mom.

The guy kneeling beside me finally removes his hands from my face and I force myself to relax, closing my eyes while Kade plays with my hair.

"You know we can't stay here, right?" he whispers to me, using his free hand to slide his fingers through mine.

"I know."

"You won't be able to finish school."

"I don't care about school," I admit, breathing out a humorless laugh. "I hate this fucking town, Kade. I hate this house. I hate these *people*," I tell him, not missing the several disgusted looks thrown our way from across the room. "I just wanna go."

"To the second gayest city in the country?"

I smile and he lifts my fingers to his mouth, looking up when Veronica walks over to stand in front of us. Her brows dip and she bounces her eyes between me and my brother, her confusion written all over her face while she stares at our joined hands. I swallow and shrink away from her, but I don't move, terrified she's about to find the knife and the burner phone stashed in Kade's jacket beneath my head.

"Boys…" she starts, opening her mouth just to snap it shut again. "Your mom—"

"Isn't here," Kade finishes for her, locking his jaw as he speaks through his teeth. "Don't talk shit about something you know nothing about."

She blinks at him and twists her lips from side to side, thankfully dropping it while she shoves her hands into her pockets. "Are you leaving?"

We don't answer that.

She sighs heavily and backs away from us, smiling sadly before she follows the rest of her colleagues to the door. I can tell she wants to say more, but we're both eighteen and free to do whatever we want, and she knows there's nothing she can do to stop us.

"Just… tell me one thing."

"What?"

"How long have you been, you know…"

"Fucking," Kade offers, smirking when he catches the look on her face, taunting her with his eyes while he kisses each of my knuckles. "You wanna know if my baby brother was legal the first time I fucked him?"

"Jesus," she mutters, her lip curling as she fights to control her features. "Do I even want to know?"

"Get out, Veronica."

She rolls her eyes at that, and then she's gone. The front door closes behind her and I relax a little more, whining when Kade moves out from under me to help me up to my feet. He locks every door and window there is, then he takes me upstairs and wraps his arms around me from behind, staying just like that while I pull my dick out to take a piss, the weirdo.

"You know I can—"

"No."

I chuckle and shake my head at him, ignoring the sight of my own reflection while I shuffle along to wash my hands at the bathroom counter. Once I'm done, he sets me down on the edge of his bed and grabs a couple duffel bags from his closet, tossing his clothes inside before he reaches up to the top shelf. He finds the pile of cash he's been saving for two years and shoves it into one of the side pockets, then he disappears for a few seconds and comes back with his arms full of my hoodies and a bunch of other shit. I pick up one of the photos on the bed and run my finger over my mom's face, smiling to myself when I catch him tossing my eyeliner into his bag.

"Can I have that for a second?"

His eyes hit mine and he passes it to me, watching me closely while I use the camera on my phone to put it on. It's not perfect, but I'm tired as shit and this is the best I can do. I blink up at him and he licks his lips, carefully leaning over me to take my face in his hands.

"So fucking beautiful," he praises, and then he kisses me, hungry and deep as if he can't get enough.

I moan and open my mouth for him, whining again when he pulls away from me and gets back to work.

"Asshole."

He smirks and quickly finishes packing, then he takes me down to the truck and lifts me up to the passenger side. I shiver all over and he climbs up to sit beside me, pulling my seatbelt over my chest before he wraps me up in a fluffy throw blanket. My lips split into a grin and I look out through the windshield, my face falling when I spot Skully walking towards us with his head down low and his hands shoved into the pockets of his coat.

"What's he doing here?"

"I asked him to come."

"What? Why?"

"Because you need more drugs," he explains, hopping down to meet him next to the driver's side.

Skully tries to bump his fist and frowns when Kade ignores the gesture, his eyes widening when he gets a look at me. "Fucking hell, Nicky—"

"Don't look at him," Kade cuts in, tossing some cash into his hand before he takes what he's paying for.

Skully looks away and Kade lifts the bag up to his eye level, checking it for a second before he takes one of the pills out. He passes it over and Skully scoffs, looking a little taken aback when he realizes what he wants.

"What, man, you don't trust me now?"

Kade stares at him and Skully shakes his head, tossing the pill into his mouth to prove it won't do anything to him. He makes a show of swallowing it and Kade narrows his eyes, still watching him while he lights a cigarette and reaches over to give it to me.

"Are you two going somewhere?" Skully asks, side-eyeing the bags in the back, sighing when Kade ignores him again. "When are you coming back?"

"We're not."

His brows jump and he bravely glances between the two of us, opening and closing his mouth a few times as if he's struggling to find words. "So, it's true, then?" he finally asks, discreetly looking around to check no one'll hear him. "You and Nicky, you're… *together*?"

Kade cocks his head and Skully licks his teeth, laughing to himself while he backs away from us.

"You're a sick motherfucker, Rivers," he calls out,

grinning while he shoves his hands back into his pockets. "I'll probably miss you a little bit."

Kade waits for him to leave and then climbs back up to the driver's seat, swinging the door shut before he presses the button to lock us inside. I pass him the cigarette and rest my head on his shoulder, watching the lights on the dash while he drives us away from the only town we've ever known.

He doesn't look back.

He doesn't mention Arianna or Elle or any other person we know.

He just wraps his arm around me and hits the highway.

Fucking finally.

A LITTLE WHILE LATER, I YAWN AND BLINK MY EYES OPEN, wiping my mouth with the back of my hand before I swallow the next pill he feeds me. He passes me a bottle of water and I take it, rolling my eyes when he drops a small ham and cheese sandwich on my lap.

"Eat."

"My throat hurts."

"Your ass'll hurt if you don't do as you're told."

"Because you'll fuck it or smack it?"

He snorts and unwraps the packet for me, keeping one eye on the road while he lifts it up to my lips.

"Can we get married someday?" I ask randomly, speaking around my food.

"No."

"Can we have kids?"

"Fuck, no."

"Can we have a cat?"

"A *cat*?" he echoes, scrunching his nose at me with his head pulled back. "Why can't you ask me for a fuckin' dog like a normal person?"

"Because I like cats."

He sighs heavily and scrubs a hand over the side of his face, nodding while he takes the next exit off the highway. "Fine, you can have a cat."

"*We.*"

"*You,*" he argues. "*Your* cat."

I grin like a dumbass, and he spends the next fifteen minutes looking for a hotel for us to sleep in. He gets me the biggest bed he can find and gently removes the clothes from my body, then he lies down between my open legs and sucks the cum from my dick, just like he told me he would.

CHAPTER 25

PRESTON

Thirty four years old…

I've waited four years for this day to come.

For four fucking years, I've paced every inch of this cell and daydreamed of all the ways I could do it:

Lie him out like a starfish… bend him over on his hands and knees… hold him upside down by his ankles and watch the blood drain from his open mouth…

So many wonderful possibilities.

After a few more minutes of pacing and daydreaming, the bright lights finally fill the block and I look up, smiling happily when my cell door opens for shower time.

You better make it hurt, man. You better make him beg or we'll come in there and we'll make you beg.

I can't have that, now, can I?

I know all about what my nephew did to those high

school boys, and I'd rather not have to swallow my own tongue when prison food is so much tastier.

Michael follows me out and falls in line beside me, rolling his big brown eyes when he catches the look on my face. "Do you have to do that?"

"Do what?"

"Be so happy all the time," he answers. "It annoys me."

"That's because you're a moody asshole," I tease him, stopping abruptly when I get to my brother-in-law's cell. "Good morning, Officer Rivers!" I sing loudly, just like I've done every morning for the last three months, chuckling when he rams his shoulder into mine. "Just *morning*, then? Without the *good*?"

He glares at the nasty looks he's getting and carries on walking, rudely ignoring me while he makes his way down the stairs. I sigh dramatically and skip to catch up with him, wrapping my arm around his shoulder while I guide him towards the bathroom we share with seventy two other inmates. He tries to shove me off of him and Michael shoves him from behind, so hard that he falls and smacks his nose on the concrete.

"Oh, dear." I feign concern, grabbing his elbow to pull him back up to his feet. "Michael, that wasn't very nice."

My cell mate lets out a rare, quiet laugh and takes his other elbow, easily picking him up to help me carry him to the showers. Eric struggles and kicks his legs out from beneath him, grunting when Michael turns and rams his knee into his balls. He drops to the floor and I kick him down on his back, pouting a little bit when he does nothing but stare at the filthy ceiling above him.

"You're so boring," I complain, crouching down over his hips to study the dark bruises all over his face.

Me and my friends have been bullying him like this since he got here and I've never gotten a rise out of him, but today… today I *will* get a rise out of him.

"I mean, you're even more boring than Michael is, and living with Michael is like living with a brick wall."

Nothing.

"Well, five brick walls instead of four, you know?"

I swear to god he's not even listening at this point.

I sigh again and straighten up to my full height, keeping my feet either side of his waist while I reach over to turn the water on. "I talked to your boys last night."

He blinks at that, his big head whipping to the side when one of the younger guys *trips* over his face. "Shit, sorry, Officer!" he calls out, playing with his soft dick while he starts the shower next to mine.

I snort and shake my head at him, raising a cocky ass brow when I look down to find Eric's eyes on me.

Well, well, well…

"They say *fuck you*, by the way," I joke, grinning when I catch the look on his face, his eyes darkening with something that looks an awful lot like rage.

"Where are they?"

"On some beach in Cali, I think."

"What the fuck are they doing in California?"

"Why do you care?"

"They're the reason I'm in here, you dumb shit," he spits out. "They set me up."

"Yeah, so you keep saying," I mutter, stepping back to make room for Michael and the other two guys. "But let's say that's true for a second… can you really blame them? You made them miserable, man. You fucked those boys up so bad they thought it was okay to fuck each other."

His lip curls and he shudders, thrashing his elbows about when we pull him up off the floor and toss him into the freezing cold water coming down from the shower head. I wrap my hands around his throat and shove him back against the wall, my own lip curling in disgust while I move my eyes over his form.

"I can't figure out what my sister ever saw in you."

"Your sister was a stupid little cunt."

"Is that right?" I laugh, taking the heavy pipe Michael slips me to smash it into the side of his head.

His knees hit the tiles and I hit him again, enjoying the way the blood flies from his head the way candy flies from a piñata. The four of us crowd his space and the guards I'm friends with do nothing, standing off to the side with their eyes on us while my other friends strip the clothes from Eric's body. Despite the big gash in his head, he keeps struggling and then *finally* tries to fight us off, looking up at me with a splash of fear in his dark blue eyes.

"What are you doing?"

I shrug nonchalantly and rest my weapon on my shoulder, bending my knees to bring my face down to his level. "Did you know I made a deal with your sons a couple years ago?" I whisper, smirking like a bad moth-erfucker when his brows dip in confusion.

"What deal?"

"It's quite simple, really," I tell him, hanging my arms over the pipe on either side of my head. "I gave them my truck… and they gave me *you*. Isn't that nice?"

"Preston."

"Eric."

"Don't—"

"I'm sorry, what?" I shout over the voices, squinting at him while I lift a hand to my ear. "I can't hear you over all these men searching for a good *pussy* to fill."

He growls at me and Michael flips him over onto his stomach, ripping the orange pants from his legs before he kneels down behind him. I tilt my head to the side and watch him pull out his massive forearm of a cock, wincing on purpose while I study Eric's hairy asshole.

"How on earth are you going to fit all that in there?"

He ignores my very valid question and the other two pin my sister's killer with their knees on his shoulders, laughing like maniacs while they beat his face and back.

"*Fuck*!" Eric shouts, puking all over the drain, his face turning an awful shade of green. "No! *No*! Preston, get him off me! Get him the fuck *off*—"

I kick him in the face to shut him up and watch them take it in turns, *without* lube because, well, I don't have any on me right now, but also because fuck this asshole. *Literally.* I want him to *feel* the way they tear him in two. I hope it burns like a bitch, and I hope he burns in hell for all the pain he inflicted on my sister.

He broke her fucking spirit, killed her brain and crushed her into a shell of the girl she used to be.

He crushed her *skull* on her own goddamn counter.

And now I'm going to crush his.

"*Preston!*" he screams, his high pitched voice cracking at the end. "Preston, *please. Please*, make it s-stop."

"You wanna die already?"

"Yes."

"Are you *sure*?"

"*Yes!*" he cries, his teeth chattering at the icy cold water raining down on him, his tears soaking his face as his mouth pools with blood. "Yes, I'm s-sure."

I click my tongue at him and let him suffer for another minute or twelve, then I lift my arm up and smash my pipe into his temple. *Repeatedly*. Again and again until my muscles start to ache. My nephew's voice fills my left ear and I roll my eyes at the demanding bastard, dropping the steel to the floor to prop my free hand on my waist.

"It's done," I tell them into the phone, breathing hard because *fuck me*, killing someone burns a lot more calories than I thought it would. "You're welcome."

EPILOGUE

KADE

TWENTY THREE YEARS OLD…

"THIS IS SOME BULLSHIT," NICKY MUTTERS, RUNNING HIS bratty little mouth all the way out to the street.

"What's wrong with you?"

"I'm *holding your hand*, Kade," he informs me, half flicking his cup towards the busy coffee shop we just left. "I'm wearing your goddamn *t-shirt* and that bitch was just eye fucking you right in front of me."

"What bitch?"

His eyes narrow and I roll my lips together, snatching his wrist when he moves like he's about to walk away from me.

"Hey—"

"Do you still like girls?" he blurts out, his cheeks heating as I back him up into the wall of the bar we moved into three months ago.

"I like you."

"That's not what I asked."

I smirk a little bit and drag the huge t-shirt up to his waist, still holding my coffee while I run my fingers over his navel. "No, baby, I don't like girls," I admit, leaning over him to catch his bottom lip between my teeth. "I like *your* mouth. *Your* body. *Your* tight little hole…" I taunt, moving my hand around to his ass to pull his hips up to mine. "You gonna give it to me?"

He nods and I kiss him, enjoying the way he still shivers for me despite the fact it's hot as shit out here. The sun is just starting to set and the streets are bursting with people, the white noise of their voices filling my ears as they pass us on the sidewalk behind me. They're probably staring at the way we're all but dry fucking against this brick wall, but I don't stop touching him, passing him my cup to free my other hand, taking his face to run my thumbs over the black makeup beneath his eyes.

Jasper was right about him.

It's been five years, and even though he's not any bigger than he was back in high school, he's so much fucking hotter.

It's infuriating.

Just as I think it, his attention wanders to something over my shoulder and I follow his line of sight, locking my jaw when I catch the young blond guy watching me and my brother. He sees me looking and quickly looks away, his shoulders bunching up to his ears as he pretends to search for something on his passenger seat.

"Kade…" Nicky says, and I shake my head, already knowing what he's thinking without having to ask.

"I already told you no."

"Dude, he's homeless."

"He doesn't look homeless to me," I argue, not missing his pretty boy haircut or his designer clothes or the fifty thousand dollar Audi he's sitting in.

"He's been sleeping in that car for three days, Kade," Nicky argues back, pulling me down by my neck to stick his pouty bottom lip out. "Please, just talk to him."

I let out a sound crossed between a sigh and a growl, glaring at him for a solid minute before I move to do as he asked. "You and your fucking strays."

He grins at the mention of his ugly ass cat and I knock on the roof of the Audi. The kid jumps so hard he almost smacks his head on the rear-view, opening and closing his mouth a couple times as he rolls the window down.

"I…"

"Come inside," I tell him, tilting my head at the bar before I guide Nicky through the main doors.

I don't know if he'll follow or not considering he looks terrified I'm about to kick his ass, but if he doesn't man up and come in here, I'm not fucking chasing him.

Less than a minute later, he carefully walks inside and looks around, avoiding our eyes while he studies the dusty black walls and the chairs stacked up on the tops of the tables. We finally bit the bullet a few months ago, sold the cabin we haven't been to in years and used the cash to buy this place. We're not open yet because it's still a shit hole, even after three weeks of constant work being done, but it's *our* shit hole and we like it.

The blond guy clears his throat and shoves his hands into the pockets of his shorts, clearly unsure where to put himself. "Look, I'm sorry if I'm not allowed to park—"

"Sit down."

He blinks at my tone but does as he's told, awkwardly dropping his ass onto one of the stools in front of the bar. We walk around to the other side and I take a bottle of whiskey from the box on the floor, grabbing three clean glasses to set them down in front of him.

"I'm Nicky and that's Kade," Nicky offers, tossing our empty to-go cups in the trash. "What's your name?"

"Cameron," he answers, relaxing a little bit at my brother's sweet demeanor.

I fight a glare and twist the cap off, holding my hand out while I pour us all a drink each. "You're twenty one?"

He nods and pulls his wallet from his pocket, still avoiding eye contact with me while he passes me the card. I scan it for his date of birth and then give it to Nicky, gently running my hand over the back of his neck while he leans over to grab his laptop. He shivers again and flips it open, pushing his ass back into my thigh while he taps away on his keyboard. Cameron's brows dip but he doesn't ask questions, proving he's not as stupid as I thought he'd be.

"Are you still in school?" I ask, deliberately playing with my baby's hair while I pass him a glass.

"Yeah, I… I'm a junior on a partial scholarship but my parents just stopped paying for my apartment."

"What are you studying?"

"Football," Nicky answers for him, making him frown.

"How did you know that?"

"Lucky guess," he says vaguely, biting his lip when I move my hand down to his waist.

"Why'd your parents cut you off?"

"Because they caught me fucking a boy," Cameron mutters, clearing his throat when my eyes hit his. "I mean, actually, *I* was the one getting—"

"Stop talking."

"Sorry."

Nicky laughs to himself and dips his head, discreetly nodding at me once he's finished his checks. I hesitate for a few seconds and he kicks my ankle, widening his eyes with a look that says *do it or I will.*

The things I do for this fucking boy.

"You need a job?"

"Um, yeah, actually. I've applied everywhere but—"

"You ever worked in a bar before?"

"No, but I'm a fast learner."

I search his eyes and swallow the last of my drink, tilting my head towards Nicky while I set my glass back down between us. "You think he's hot?"

"I…" he trails off, blushing a little bit as he looks at Nicky for help. "Dude, what's the right answer?"

Nicky hides a grin and I slide my fingertips over the curve of his spine, raising a brow while I wait for Cameron to tell me yes or no.

"Uh, no—I mean, sure, I guess, but I'm a bottom so… I think *you're*… hot," he finally finishes, wincing at Nicky when he catches the look on my face. "That wasn't the right answer, was it?"

"Nope."

He chews his lip and I take the spare set of keys from my pocket, surprising them both when I toss them into Cameron's hand. "Go grab yourself some food if you haven't eaten already. Get all your shit from your car and lock both doors behind you. There's another studio upstairs you can crash in until you find your own place. Meet us down here at eight tomorrow morning so Nicky can put you on the books."

"Wait, that's it?" he calls, frowning again while he watches us move for the door leading to the stairs.

"Do you have any questions?"

"No, I just… thank you for this. I *really* appreciate it."

"Yeah, well, if you turn into a shady fucker or try to hurt my little brother, I'll throw you off the roof."

"Your what?"

"The *roof*," Nicky exaggerates, laughing again when Cameron stares at us with his mouth parted.

I smirk and wrap my arms around Nicky's waist, licking the side of his neck while I take him upstairs. I quickly unlock the door on my left and push him through it, popping the button on his ripped jeans before I shove him down on the bed in the corner.

"You think he can be trusted?" I ask, kneeling on the mattress between his thighs to work on his zipper.

"I think you like him."

"I don't *like* anyone, Nicky."

"But me," he reminds me, lifting his ass up to help me out. "You like me, right?"

I strip his clothes off but leave the t-shirt, sliding my hands over the tattoos on his forearms to pin his wrists above his head. He locks his thighs around me and I grind on him slowly, fucking my hard dick against his to show him just how much I *like* him.

"Spread your legs out."

He does as he's told and I pull his bottom lip into my mouth, letting go of his arms to move my hands down to his sides. He sucks in a breath and I squeeze his waist, fucking loving the way I can make him moan for me on cue. He scrapes his black nails over my scalp and I dig my thumbs into his hip bones, nudging his chin to the side to get to his neck. I don't think Cameron was lying to me about being a bottom, but it won't hurt to mark him just in case, to show him who my boy belongs to.

"Kade," he pleads, rubbing himself against the front of my jeans. "You're taking too long."

I dig my teeth in even harder and he whines, but he doesn't try to pull away from me. His legs start to shake and he presses his heels into my ass, whimpering when I smack his outer thigh.

"I said out."

"Fuck, you're killing me."

I grin against him and lift my head to get a look at his throat, my eyes darkening as I move them over the several purple hickeys I've given him. It's not enough, but he's getting desperate and impatient, so I'll just have to leave him be and finish later when he's asleep.

"There's something wrong with you," he tells me, and I nod, sliding down to move my lips over his abs.

He's right—because he's always fucking right—but there's not much I can do about it now.

I knew taking him once would be the death of me and I did it anyway. I was naïve, and I thought I'd start to get my sanity back as the years went on, but my love for him only gets worse, *more* toxic and *more* selfish.

It's unfortunate and unhealthy as fuck, but he doesn't mind as much as he's letting on.

He likes me crazy.

I lick the smooth spot just above the base of his cock and he jerks beneath me, his breath coming in a little faster as I push his knees out either side of his ribs. He looks down at me and I hold his eyes, spitting on his pale little hole before I flick it with my tongue. He moans again and I pull his cheeks out with my thumbs, greedily eating him out for as long as I damn well please. After a while, he rips his hands over his face and I decide to put him out of his misery, blindly reaching up to grab the lube we keep in the nightstand.

"Tell me how many."

"Just one," he rasps. "Don't give me all of it."

"Good boy," I whisper, pushing my wet finger in to the second knuckle, still licking his hole while I crook it upwards. "Fuck it back for me."

He rolls his hips up and I use my left hand to get my jeans and boxers down to my thighs, rubbing the lube all over my dick to get it ready for him. I spit on him a few more times and slide my knees up to his ass, removing my finger to replace it with the head of my cock. His mouth parts as I push it inside, but he doesn't complain. He's half my size and he takes my dick like it's *nothing*, like he was made for me and *only* me.

No one but me.

I place my elbows either side of his head and drop my mouth to his, tangling our tongues together while I fuck it all into him. His tiny hands find my waist and he pushes my shirt up, waiting for me to move back before he pulls it all the way off. He throws it on the floor and moves his hands down to my ass, pulling me in like he's fixing for me to fuck him even harder.

"Like this?" I ask, eagerly giving him what he's so needy for. "What do you want, baby?"

"Will you let me ride it?"

"No."

"Please," he begs, and I raise a brow at him, rolling us over until I'm on my back and he's on top.

His eyes light up and he bites his lip, smacking my hands away when I move to grab his waist.

Oh, fuck, no.

"Don't play with me, Nicky," I taunt, but he's already acting up like the brat he is, his tongue trapped between his teeth as he leans over and teases my nose with his.

"I wanna play."

"What's the game?"

"Easy," he whispers, snatching a pillow to shove it beneath my head. "I bet you fifty bucks you won't let *me* fuck *you* until we both come."

I smirk and he smirks back, taking my wrists to pin them to the sheet above me.

"Don't move."

I lick my lips and he sits up on my lap, moving his hungry little eyes over my form while he drags his nails from my chest to my abs. I groan and he shushes me—fucking *shushes* me like he'd shush a wild animal—then he leans over me again to wrap five warm fingers around my throat.

"Good boy," he says simply, and I swear to god I almost lose before he's even started.

He grins at the look on my face and straightens back up, my t-shirt covering his ass as he fucks himself on my dick. I look down between us and he looks down, too, fisting the hem of the fabric to pull it up to his collarbone. He slowly rolls his hips back and forth, teasing the shit out of us both, and then the fucker moans on purpose, his head falling back on his shoulders as he twists and pinches his own nipples. I grit my teeth and curl my toes into the blanket, my fingers flexing above my head as I watch him—

Fuck this.

"No—*Kade!*" he screams, laughing at me when I flip him over until he's back where he belongs.

I rip my jeans the rest of the way off and take my wallet from my pocket, shoving the cash into his open hand while I slide my cock back inside him. He moans for real this time and I fuck him hard and deep, pulling his jaw down with my thumb to eat the inside of his mouth.

"I fucking love this hot little mouth," I tell him. "The way you taste… you're so fucking sweet."

He nods like he knows it and I pull his head back by

his hair, riding him even harder when I hear the sound of keys turning in the lock next door.

"Louder, baby," I rasp, sliding my hands through his to lock our fingers together, pinning them to the bed either side of his face. "Tell me you're mine."

"I'm yours," he rushes out. "I'm yours, I'm yours, I'm fucking... *fuck*!"

"You gonna come for me?"

"*Yes*," he gasps, squirming and fighting beneath me, frowning when I shake my head and keep holding him down.

"No hands."

"Shit, Kade, I *can't*."

"Yes, you can," I tease, tilting my hips out to grind on him the way he likes it. "Relax, baby. Calm your ass down and let me fuck it out of you."

He whimpers but does his best to obey me, his black eyebrows scrunching together in concentration, forming that sexy little vee just above his nose. I nip his pretty lips and lick his tongue, enjoying myself a lot more than I should be while I make him work for it. It takes him a minute, but he finally tenses against me and lifts his ass all the way up, screaming my name into my mouth while his cum shoots out from the tip of his dick and covers us both.

Fuck me, that's hot.

My cock throbs at the feel of him and I fill him up at the same time, digging my fingertips into his knuckles while our bodies shake and writhe together. As soon as we're both done, the back of his head hits the pillow and I drop mine next to it, slowly pulling out to lie down beside him. I bring his back to my chest and run my hand over his hip, drawing light circles there while I listen to him breathe. It gradually evens out and I watch him fall asleep, the same way I've been watching him every night since the day I found him on that locker room floor five years ago. He hasn't had a nightmare or a panic attack in just over six months, but I'm constantly terrified they're about to come back and torment him all over again.

I can't remember the last time I wasn't terrified for him.

I kiss his hairline and reach up to scratch the cat's chin, wincing through my teeth when he digs his razor sharp claws into my head. His name is Teddy, because Nicky took one look at him at the shelter and said he looked like a tiny gray teddy bear. I said he looked like a fucking rat, but here we are.

I bat him away from me and he hisses, the little prick, walking along the pillow to curl up next to my brother. I flip him off and Nicky takes my hand, laughing at me while he moves it back to his hip. My eyes narrow and I drop my mouth to his neck, sliding my wet cock over his hole to push it back inside him. He makes a choking noise and I pull his head back on my shoulder, gently fucking him again while I lick the vein beneath my lips.

"Go back to sleep, baby boy," I whisper, sucking his soft flesh into my mouth. "I got you."

He relaxes against me and I drag his thigh out over my waist, smiling to myself while I rub his dick and mark his body for all to see.

My brother.

My best friend.

My entire fucking world.

And this right here… the two of us living in our own shitty apartment above our shitty bar with our shitty looking rat for a cat… *this* is our forever.

The End.

ACKNOWLEDGMENTS

To my husband and sons, I love you so much.

To my beautiful friends and family, for being awesome enough to stick by me through four books and counting. I know I'm lucky to have a support system like this one, and I couldn't do this without you.

To Mum and Lisa, for encouraging me to take risks, to be who I am, and to write what I love.

To Megan, my lil Kade, who knows this book better than I do. I adore you and all the random Dirty Love quotes you send me.

To my book besties, my author besties, my blogger besties, my reader besties… there are too many of you to name, but I just wanted to say thank you for the endless love and friendship and support. I adore you bishes.

To my designer, Haya, for this stunning cover. You're amazing and I'm keeping you forever.

To my incredible readers group. You know how hard this book was for me to write, and if you made it this far, I suppose now you know why. Thank you for your excitement for Kade and Nicky, for encouraging me to keep going, and for watching me bawl my eyes out. I'm still mortified, but I love you all anyway.

To my amazing ARC team and street team, you

know what you did. Thank you for reading and reviewing and promoting the crap out of this book. For staying up until the early hours of the morning to talk about it with me. For helping me make this story the best it could be. For loving Kade and Nicky as much as I do. For losing your damn minds and threatening to kidnap me. I love you all from the bottom of my heart, even when you drive me crazy.

And to you, the reader on the other side of this page, thank you for taking a chance on me and this book.

All my love,
Bethany <3

ALSO BY BETHANY WINTERS

The Kingston Brothers

Kings of Westbrook High

Reckless at Westbrook High

Joker Night

Nightmare

Hawthorne University

Like You Hate Me

Standalones

Little Devil

Dirty Love

ABOUT THE AUTHOR

Bethany lives in South Wales with her husband and their two boys. She loves iced coffee, books, big hoodies, and Machine Gun Kelly, although her husband is still pretty mad about that last one. When she's not writing, she's either daydreaming about all the crazy characters inside her head, reading, getting coffee, or raiding bookstores for pretty paperbacks to hoard.

Join Bethany Winters' Book Baddies to be the first to know about anything and everything Bethany related.

Sign up for her newsletter to receive (irregular) updates on what she's reading and writing about, early teasers, new releases, bonus scenes, giveaways, and more: https://bethanywinters.co.uk/subscribe